Chi-Town Hood Affairs

By Nicole Black

Dedication

Grandma,

You were....

The strongest woman I have ever met.

You were....

A woman that touched the lives of many.

You were....

A savior to those in need.

You are....

An angel now.

Mrs. Inez Jackson, I didn't hear you all those times you said, "get up off your narrow a** and do something with yourself." Now that you're gone, I find it crazy that I hear you loud and clear. I took that advice and it landed me in a position to write this message. Hopefully you're looking down on me with pride in your eyes. May you continue to rest in peace.

Acknowledgments

I thank God for giving me this talent that I didn't know existed within me until I hit a rough patch in life. God really works in mysterious ways.

Jinnie Jackson, I LOVE YOU!!! No words can describe how much I appreciate all you do for me. You are the definition of a STRONG WOMAN! I wouldn't trade you for the world. Thanks for being you!

Jamari; the only man that I'll do anything for. Watching you grow up is the best experience I'll ever experience. I love you son, always.

Tammy, Carolyn, Kris, Michael, Breard, Erick, Zack, Shun, Raymond, Lyric, Peanut, Moo-Moo, Aaron, and the rest of my family, all of you mean a lot to me. If I never said it before I'm saying it now, I love y'all!!

To my homie Steve, my "lil sis" Shamarco, and my homegirl Mallory, thank you for taking the time out to read this book when it was just paged on my laptop. I appreciate the feedback and push from y'all. James and Vicky, both of y'all truly are great friends. I don't know what I'd do without y'all. J-baby, since we've met you have only said positive things to me and about me. I'm glad to have someone like you in my life. You are the best!

My self-proclaimed #1 supporter, Eric. You already know where we stand. I love you to death; nothing else has to be said. Brandon, without you giving me that extra push, I never would have chased my dream. Thank you for that and for always bringing positive energy to the room!

Dee, you are an exceptional man that all men can learn something from. Before you really got to know me you looked out for me in a way that I could never repay you for. Ever since that day you have continued to look out for me out of pure kindness. Words can't express how much I love you and appreciate everything you do for me. I will forever be grateful to have you in my life.

Tiff, Dominique, Shun, Shevitta, Nita, Mike, Larry, Cardell, Linda, and my day 1's, Shunta, Tasia, and Meechi, thanks for all of the support you give me and for always being there for me. All of y'all are stuck with me for life. Special thanks to Meechi for lending me your name for the series.

I would like to give a very special thank you to the one and only Shan! You are one admirable woman. Thank you for inspiring me and giving me this opportunity. To the talented ladies of Shan Presents and the men and women of The Bankroll Squad, I wish each and every one of you much success as you go on this journey.

Thanks to everyone that worked on, bought, read, borrowed, supported, and promoted this book. From the bottom of my heart I appreciate it.

Text SHAN to 22828 to keep up with new releases, contest, sneak peeks from Shan and the ladies of Shan Presents

Cola

"You got some work?" I asked the man that stood on the block while looking at the ground with my hat low, covering my eyes, because I was ashamed of myself. He looked me up and down; probably wondering why in the hell was I asking him that. "I'm not the police," I said as I felt him eyeing me carefully. I looked down at the black and red Air Max 95's I had on, and then thought about the brand new, black True Religion jeans and black and red Northface hoodie I wore. I was too damn clean to be a crack head.

He walked closer to me and said, "Tell me you out here buyin' this shit for a sick ass family member." A tear fell from my eye. I tried to wipe it before he saw it hit the ground. I wasn't quick enough. "Damn, you lookin' for somethin' to numb some type of pain and I ain't gon' help you wit' that."

As I stood there, more tears came because he was right, that's exactly what I wanted, something to numb my pain. I finally looked up. He looked exactly the same, except he wasn't as skinny as he was before. He stood six feet two inches, had the thickest eyebrows, and longest eyelashes. He had dark skin with the most innocent eyes.

I wonder when he smiled, did that one dimple he hated so much still show. I laughed when I thought about how he used to say it made him look soft.

Here I was, standing on the corner, trying to buy dope from a man I used to love. *I hope he didn't know who I was*; I thought as I walked away. Quickly, I let go of that notion; if he did he would have said something.

I walked towards State Street to head home. I looked at the dirt-covered ground where the projects once were and missed those days. "Halfway home," I said to myself. I felt like I'd been walking forever. "WHAT THE HELL?!?!" I yelled when I heard tires screech in front of me.

No one got out of the black Dodge Charger for a few minutes. I decided to continue on my walk while looking out the corner of my eye. When I moved, the car moved. When I stopped, the car stopped. This went on for three blocks.

Fed up, I picked up several rocks and threw them at the car. The car door swung open and boy did I regret throwing those rocks. Scared to death, I wanted to run, but my feet wouldn't work.

I heard a voice say, "Did you honestly think I was gon' sell that shit to you?" Embarrassed, I tried to walk away, but felt a tight grip on my arm. "What the fuck is goin' on wit' you? Why you tryin' to buy dope? Talk to me." I stood there unable to look at him. The last time I saw him it wasn't a good memory. "So you not gon' talk to me? I looked for you for two years before I gave up. You just up and left me for dead."

"Huh? Left you for dead?"

"Yeah I got shot in the chest, I needed you."

After my brother called and told me Zell had been shot, I went on with my life, I didn't care who shot him or why. "Zell, you did so much shit to me over the years. The last straw was when you fucked a bitch in our bed. A bed I slept in next to you every night. That hurt me to the core."

He looked down and said, "My bad." Next thing I knew I had slapped him. I thought about the day I walked in the house and saw him and some woman lying naked in our bed. His dick was all shriveled up with dried up sex juices on it. This bastard didn't even use a condom. His eyes got big as he grabbed his face, his eyes softened as he looked at me. "Aight, I deserved that, it was a long time comin'. You got that, but why didn't you come to the hospital?"

I could see the pain in his eyes. "I--I----Ummmmm." I couldn't think of a lie fast enough. Finally I said, "At the time, I hated you for hurting me. I wanted you to hurt like I was hurting." He looked mad, but it was the truth.

Staring at my slanted, dark brown eyes, he spoke calmly, "Enough about the past, Cola." Cola was a nickname my brother Jay gave me when we were teenagers because I was brown skinned with dyed red hair. It made sense to me. "We crossed paths with each other for a reason. I don't like the reason much, but I'm glad it happened. We need to go somewhere and have a long talk, maybe you will tell me what's wrong."

"Honestly, I don't want to share that with you right now. We can go to my house to talk, if you not busy."

"I got nothin' but time for you. Get in the car, I gotta go back to the block and let my homie know I'mma be out of reach for the rest of the day."

We turned on the block. Zell got out of the car to talk to a couple of young boys that were standing there. He left his white iPhone on the charger in the car and it began to vibrate. I ignored it. It stopped and began to vibrate again, this time I looked at it. It was a text from a female. I read the text: *Hey baby I'm home just thinking about you I'm sorry about the things I said, just come home or call me at least. We need to talk.* I deleted the text because I had plans for Zell, whoever this Anaya was would only be in the way.

Just as I was about to put the phone down, Zell was getting back in the car. "What you doin' with my phone?"

"I thought I lost my phone. I guess it fell out my pocket when I got in the car. It was on the side of the seat. Check the call log if you don't believe me."

Zell looked at his phone then back at me. "Let me see yo' call log." Zell inspected my phone like it was part of a crime scene. Without saying a word, he handed it back to me. Luckily for me, I was smart; I called my phone from his phone just in case I got caught.

Zell just drove, he never asked me where I lived or anything. I could tell something was bothering him. "Ummmm, are you okay?" I asked Zell as he drove down Lake Shore Drive.

"I'm cool," Zell replied.

"Where are we going? I thought we were going back to my house to talk."

"We goin' to talk. I got a spot up here wit' a nice view. I think it would help soothe whatever you goin' through right now."

We pulled up to a white high-rise building. The building was nice; everybody had their own balcony. The elevator was gold with mirrors, a far cry from the piss and garbage filled elevators we used to ride. "This is nice," I mumbled, more to myself than Zell. We stepped off the elevator onto the eighth floor. The hallway had red carpet. I could tell this was a building where only people with money lived.

Zell opened the door for me to walk in before him. I stopped to look around; the place was basically empty except for a black leather couch, a fifty-inch TV in the living room, a stove, and a fridge. I guess he read my mind because he said, "I just come here to chill sometimes." While I walked over to the floor to ceiling window he shouted, "Make yo'self at home I'll be right back." He disappeared to the back of the apartment.

The view of the water had me mesmerized. It was so dark and pretty. The waves were low and calm; it was soothing to my soul. Still, it wasn't enough to make me forget about what happened to my brother. As I began to form tears, Zell came back in the room. I buried my head in my hands to begin letting out all of my forced tears. "What am I going to do without him?" I said to no one in particular.

"What's wrong? Talk to me, Cola."

I was too hysterical to talk; my words were inaudible through all of the crying. In order to keep the fake tears coming, I had to imagine my brother's body exactly the way it was arranged for him to be killed. I thought about any and everything that had ever caused me pain. Once I got the tears going, there was no stopping this charade. Zell led me to the couch. Every tear that escaped, he wiped away with his soft hands.

"I'll be right back." I got off the couch to go to the bathroom to clean my face. As I looked in the mirror, I noticed how red and puffy my once slanted eyes were. My brown complexion no longer had the radiant glow it usually had. I looked bad as hell, but in the end it would be worth it.

I went through a lot to make this believable. Every time I put on eye shadow my eyes would get all red and puffy, I used that to my advantage this morning. I packed that shit all around my eyes and kept it on for an hour. When I wiped it off I had just enough swelling and redness to make it seem like I had been crying for days. Maybe I'd have a future as an actress after this.

As I opened the door, I jumped back; startled that Zell was standing there. "You cool?" he asked.

"Yeah, I'm good now. Thank you." I turned the TV to the sports channel to watch a basketball game. Even though Chicago was the city that I was born, raised, and resided in, I loved a different basketball team. Zell sat down to watch the game. Neither of us said a word until the game was over.

It's show time. "Zell, can we talk now?"

He looked at me with concern in his eyes. "Yeah we can."

"Earlier, I was a mess. I found my brother dead in his house two days ago. He was stabbed, shot in the heart, and had knives sticking out of his eyes. I wanted something to erase that sight out of my mind; it was too much for me. Every time I close my eyes I see his body. They didn't have to do him like that." I let tears cascade down my face.

"Damn."

"He was all I had, Zell, and somebody took him from me. He was so overprotective of me; I thought he was my daddy at times. I loved him so much. Jay was the reason I didn't have to work. He always told me as long as he was alive, I wouldn't have to depend on anybody. He kept his word. Here I am twenty-five years old, no kids, no bills, no job, and now, no Jay. He set some money to the side for me, just in case something ever happened to him. I guess he wanted to take care of me, even from his grave."

Zell's eyes filled with sorrow as he listened to me. I rocked back and forth as I thought about my baby brother, Jay, who thought he was the big brother. Zell didn't say more than one word while he listened to me talk about Jay for hours.

It took a lot for me not to cause bodily harm to this man. Him comforting me like he didn't have shit to do with the reason I was sitting in his face had me ready to kill him. Zell will get what was coming to him very soon.

Zell

"Sorry about your brother, Cola. I figured it was something deep for you to wanna get high."

Even though Cola and I ended on bad terms, I never stopped lovin' her. We had a crazy relationship. I don't know how she put up wit' me wit' all the bullshit I put her through. She was the most loyal female I had ever met. I never gave a fuck about her brother, but I was willing to be here for her through this.

I was actually smilin' on the inside because that nigga was dead. I had get rid of Anaya, my girl for the past year. She was just something to pass time anyway. Now that Cola was back around, I didn't need her.

I couldn't lie; Naya had that look. She had that smooth, dark, chocolate skin with hazel eyes and high cheekbones. She had the body of a Goddess. I'm talkin' big plump ass, nice hips, small waist, and a set of 34C's that sat up perfectly. The long, black weave she wore was always perfect.

Naya was cool, but at times she got on my nerves. She thought just because she was pretty the world owed her somethin'. In all honesty, all she was really good for was arm candy and sex. Even the sex wasn't that great. I hated I got her pregnant. I tried to make her get rid of it, but she wasn't goin' for that. I wish I could erase what happened when Cola was pregnant. Now Naya was about to do what Cola should have done years ago, have my child.

Cola and Naya were like night and day. Cola was down to earth, while Naya thought she owned the earth. Naya had the perfect body and Cola had flaws that she wore well. I loved that. Cola was tall, at least five feet ten inches, long legs, thick thighs, and a small butt.

She had very small love handles that I used to pinch and she wasn't insecure about them. She could easily hide or get rid of them. Cola chose to wear her flaws with pride that drove me crazy about her.

Cola was beautiful. Her medium, brown complexion had a glow at all times. Her slightly slanted, dark brown eyes could seduce any man that looked into them for too long. Her eyes also had a certain pain in them that made you want to know her story.

She had the fullest, prettiest lips I had ever seen. Her eyebrows were so thick and neatly arched, I used to think she permed them; they were just that perfect.

She never wore make up or weave, unlike Anaya who had to have that shit on at all times. Although her hair was dyed red, it was hers. It fell right on her shoulders. Cola was really into tattoos and had at least thirty. She was truly a natural beauty.

"Dezell King!" I snapped out of my daydream when I heard Cola call me by my government name, which I hated.

"Yeah, what's up? You good?" I asked while I looked over at her to make sure she hadn't been cryin' while I was sittin' there daydreaming.

"I'm okay. It's like three a.m. and I wanna get in my bed, plus your phone has been vibrating nonstop. I was trying to get your attention, but you were in a daze."

"I was thinkin' about some shit. You know you don't have to go nowhere; we can chill here tonight. The couch ain't hard." I laughed at that twisted up face she was givin' me. That let me know she was not tryin' to sleep on a couch with me.

"I'll sleep on the floor." She agreed to stay after I told her I was too tired to drive. That was a lie; I just didn't want her to leave.

Cola

I woke up feeling good due to the fact I accomplished what I set out to do the day before. I looked on the floor where Zell slept, but he was gone. His phone was still there, that let me know he wasn't far away. I checked the bathroom and the bedroom; he wasn't in the house.

When I walked over to the couch, his phone lit up. I picked up the phone to see he had three missed calls and a voicemail from the same chick. I deleted the calls then listened to the voicemail.

"I guess you really are pissed at me over what I said. I'm so sorry; I didn't mean it. Can you please call me so we can talk about things? I love you Zell."

After I deleted the voicemail, I carefully put the phone back on the floor in the exact same position it was in before I picked it up.

My phone began to vibrate. I answered immediately for my best friend, Kee. "Hey girl, I'm alright....I'm at his house....I'll be there soon.''

I heard keys as I hung up with Kee. Zell came in the living room with breakfast from The Pancake House. "What's up? You feelin' better this mornin'?" He handed me the white tray of food.

"Yeah, I do. Can you believe I was ten dollars away from being a crack head?" That was a rhetorical question.

He shook his head and said, "I almost didn't recognize yo' ass wit' that hat on. That tat you got on yo' finger gave you away."

I forgot about the letter J that I had tattooed on my left ring finger, in representation of the child I had lost. Boy or girl, the name was going to start with the letter J.

His phone began to vibrate again. I hope it wasn't the same girl that called earlier; I needed to figure out who she was. I listened as he talked to whoever was on the line. By the way the conversation sounded, it wasn't her. He looked stressed when he hung up the phone.

"What's wrong?" I walked over to him and massaged his shoulders as he explained what was on his mind.

"I gotta keep it one hundred wit' you." That meant trouble, he only said that when he was about to tell me something I didn't want to hear or when he was trying to get out of the dog house. "I got a girl…" he paused to look at me, "…we been together for a year. It ain't all good wit' us right now. That bitch said some off the wall shit to me the other day and I haven't talked to her since." Hearing this made it that much easier to convince him to leave her. I could tell by the way he looked at me that he was still in love with me. "Cola, she's three months pregnant."

Out of anger, I hit him upside the head with his phone and it made me to reflect on an incident from the past that caused me a lot of pain.

I thought about the baby I never got a chance to hold, kiss, or see a few years ago. Zell and I weren't getting along while I was pregnant. From the day I told him I was pregnant to a couple months after my miscarriage, we barely spoke. When we did talk, it was always an argument.

I was craving an Italian beef with cheese and hot peppers late one night. I knew Zell wouldn't go get it for me because we couldn't stand each other. He was sitting in the living room when I grabbed my keys off the table.

"Where you goin'?" he asked.

"Southtown'," was all I said.

Southtown Sub on 35th was my favorite hood restaurant for their Italian beef sandwiches. That's the only thing I ever ate from there. I walked past a group of girls I knew from around the area.

"Hey, Cola, when you gon' start showin'? How many months you is now?" Peachy shouted to me. Almost every time I talked to her I had to figure out exactly what she was saying to me. Peachy was the definition of ghetto; from her loudness to the four different colors of weave she wore.

"I'm four months, Peachy." She looked at my stomach,

which was still flat.

*"Girl, I'm is gon' help you plan the baby shower."
Truthfully, I didn't know if that was a question or a
statement. There was no way in hell Peachy was helping
me with my baby shower. After talking to Peachy, I
continued to the restaurant.*

*Southtown was crowded as hell. As small as it was,
there were at least ten people in there, mostly females. I
ordered my food, then stepped outside because it was too
many people in there for me. A group of girls came out
also. One of them was staring at me.*

*I looked over my shoulder to make sure nobody was
standing behind me. As I turned around, something hit me
in my jaw; it was too hard to be a fist. Dazed, I felt the
same pain on the opposite side. When I hit the concrete, I
saw it was a padlock. I looked up to about five girls
kicking and punching me in every body part they could. I
had no choice, but to hold my stomach while I balled up.*

*One of the girls yelled, "Move her hands off her
stomach, make her lay on her back, and hold her arms and
legs." I had heard her voice before, I just couldn't put my*

finger on where.

After the first part of the beating they put on me, I barely had energy. I didn't make it easy for them to hold me down, they had to work to make me stay still. I managed to pull a few tracks out, scratch a couple of faces, and land a few punches. It was too many of them for me to hold my own. I'm not a scary bitch, but I wasn't superwoman either.

They finally had a hold on me. The girl that ordered them to hold me down walked over to me. She never looked at me, she just placed her foot on my stomach.

"OH MY GOD!!!! PLEASE DONT DO THIS," I begged.

Still, she never looked at me. I began to cry as she slowly twisted her foot gently on my stomach, almost like her purpose was to taunt me. Her foot began to rise slowly, I knew what was about to happen next. To my surprise her foot landed on my knee.

"Aggghhh!! Please stop," I cried. She ignored my cries while she stomped my right knee repeatedly.

She turned to walk away from me and I mouthed the words, "thank God." The four girls that were holding me picked me up. I was relieved she didn't stomp my stomach.

I spoke way too soon. While I was celebrating in my head, the girl made her way back to me and before I knew it, a foot was digging deep into my stomach. I counted kick after kick after kick. My poor baby took at least six kicks. I felt my pants become wet. I hoped it was urine and not blood. A crowd had formed around us. I was so focused on my baby that I didn't notice them right away.

"My baby. My baby," I cried.

Somebody from the crowd yelled, "Aw, hell naw, shorty pregnant." Then I heard a single gunshot. I prayed I wasn't the one who'd gotten shot. All the girls and the crowd scattered like roaches when the lights came on. My damaged body was the only thing still there.

A man approached me. "Damn, you bleeding down there. If I would have known you were pregnant, I would have stopped it soon as I walked up."

All I could do was cry. I knew my baby was gone

because of all the pain I was feeling and how soaked my jeans were.

"I gotta call him." I reached for my phone. "It hurts. It hurts so bad."

The man was still by my side. "Who you wanna call?" I told him Zell's number and he looked at his phone. "You fuck wit' Zell?" I shook my head yes. "Aye, yo' girl just got jumped. She out here bleeding bad in front of Southtown. I'm about to call the ambulance...Aight hurry up." He hung up the phone to focus on me. "He on his way, a'ight."

"Thank you for staying with me."

"I would have broke it up, but shit I can't lie, my theory is let them hoes fight, no disrespect. I apologize for not stopping it, I didn't know you were pregnant."

This stranger had the nicest eyes I had ever seen. They were a bluish-gray color that I had never seen before or that I would ever forget. He talked to me until the ambulance arrived. The sound of his deep voice was very calming. When I was about to ask him his name, the ambulance came. He wished me well and we went our separate ways.

The ambulance took me to Mercy Hospital where they confirmed I had lost the baby. I was hysterical. I was grateful that Zell called Kee, without her I would have gone crazy. Not once did Zell ask me if I was okay. He only came in the room with me to ask the Doctor if he was sure I had lost the baby.

I was confused by what happened. I didn't have any problems with any females that I knew of. If I caught Zell cheating, I handled him not the female. This girl seemed determined to get rid of my baby like she had known I was pregnant before I said anything. While I was thinking about the situation, the door to my room flew open and my brother Jay walked in, visibly upset.

"Sis, you good?" I shook my head no. Jay came to sit on my bed. "What happened? Why were you out so late and where was that nigga at? Did you know them hoes? Where was you going, Serenity?" The only time Jay called me by my real name was when things were serious or he was mad at me.

"I was going to the restaurant."

He got up and paced the floor, something he did when he was thinking or mad.

"Why you ain't call me? You know I will drop everything for you and my niece."

Staring directly into his eyes I said, "I lost the baby, Jay." A look came across his face that I had never seen before. It honestly scared me to see him looking as crazy as he was.

"You bullshittin'? My niece won't get to see the light of day? Her life was taken away from her before she got a chance to live it."

I told him every detail of the fight. He asked me if I remembered what they looked like, but I could only remember the one that was staring at me before the fight. I wished I could remember more than the girl's voice that was kicking me in my stomach. I began to cry, she took the one thing that meant everything to me. I hated her for that.

After I talked to Jay, he left with Kee to make sure she got home safe. Before they left, I told both of them I would *call them in the morning because I wanted to sleep. I knew Jay like the back of my hand. He was also gon' go out to try to find out any information about what happened to me. He wanted desperately to find out who was responsible for the loss of my baby.*

I didn't know what I was having, but my mother said it was a girl, so we all went with what she said. I told her she could name my first child. She was devastated when I told her I had a miscarriage. She was going to name her Jaylah, after my father, Jaylen.

Unfortunately, my father was serving a twenty-five year jail sentence for attempted murder. He had two years left. From his prison cell, he remained close to Jay, Kee, and I. We made it our business to go see him as often as we could. Father's Day and sometime around Christmas was a must.

I woke up in the middle of the night to Zell sitting in a chair by the window.

"Let me ask you somethin'?" Not asking if I was okay,

he got straight to whatever he wanted to know. "You been fuckin' somebody else?" That caught me off guard. I'm sitting in the hospital bed, beat up, and this insensitive bastard was asking me if I had been cheating on him. Sometimes I wondered why I loved him.

"You simple son of a bitch. Are you serious right now? Look where we at. You asking me this bullshit while I'm down and out. I just lost your baby and all you worried about is if I been cheating on you. If I wasn't fucked up, I would fuck you up."

"Man you been meetin' this same nigga at Harold's on 22nd, every Friday at the same time. I wanna know what the fuck is up." He kept his eyes glued to me while I talked.

"About that, first of all, don't be following me or having Starks follow me. If you are going do it, do it right. I saw him in the parking lot every time. How you hire somebody that don't know how to be discreet when they watching somebody? Second of all, that's business. His name is Cash, he the front man for the bar Jay owns. Jay pays him on Fridays and I'm the one who drops it off. Third, do you honestly think I would meet somebody I'm

messing with at Harold's?" He just sat there looking stupid. "Oh, now you're mute. Get the fuck out Zell!"

He stood to leave. "I'm sorry Cola."

"Fuck you."

Zell had me so mad I wanted to get out of the bed and hit him dead in his Adam's apple. He was a dumb ass muthafucka for real. I wish I had enough energy to bust his head. I thought about my little baby and cried myself to sleep soon after he left.

I stopped thinking about that day when I felt the tears fall. To this day, I still think about the baby I lost. I wondered if it was really a girl or was it a boy, what it would have looked like, how it would have sounded. I hated the person that took that away from me.

Zell

I couldn't help but feel bad about tellin' Cola that Anaya was pregnant. I was the reason Cola didn't get to have my baby, our baby. I had to be honest with her about Anaya bein' pregnant though, it was only fair that she knew. Now she was sittin' here daydreamin'.

I already knew she thinkin' about the night she lost the baby. If she wouldn't have been meetin' that nigga Cash all those years ago, I would have never did what I did. True, I should have asked Cola about dude the night I saw her in the restaurant with him, instead I had somebody follow her. He confirmed that she was with the same nigga every Friday, at the same time. I thought back to that night

I made the dumbest move ever…

"She there with him right now?" I asked Starks. He was a hustler by day and a killer by night. Starks could find, follow, and kill the President without being noticed if he had to. I approached him and asked him if he remembered the girl I was with at Boog's party. I told him I needed him to follow her. "Bet, I got somethin' for that sneaky ass bitch. She ain't finna' put this baby on me."

I hung up the phone with Starks so I could text my cousin Tara.

"I got somethin' I need you and yo' girls to handle. Be available to drop everything when I call. Y'all payout will be nice."

Tara was my favorite cousin. She was a stud. She acted and dressed like a dude, sometimes I would swear she had a dick bigger than mine in her pants. That was probably why we got along so good; that and the fact that we used to compete for females before I met Cola.

When I met Cola, I slowed down. I didn't completely stop, but I definitely cut down some. Tara kept her hair braided to the back under her fitted hats. She was pretty, but she should have been a man. Tara wanted to chill a couple days after I texted her, so we went to the mall out in Chicago Ridge. After that we got some wings from the spot next door.

"What up fam? What's this you need me to do for you?" Tara asked as she stuffed her face with boneless wings. I told her about Cola cheatin' wit' some other nigga and tryin' to put the baby on me. "I don't know my dude, you goin' off yo' assumptions. Besides, I don't think she would be up in a cheap ass restaurant wit' some goofy ass nigga." Tara and Cola met each other once at my family reunion in Washington Park a while back. I knew Cola probably wouldn't remember her face.

"Just handle the shit for me. Bitches always gotta be difficult."

"Fuck you nigga. I'm tryin' to make you think about this before you do it."

"I know what I wanna do." I gave Tara specific instructions on how I wanted the shit to go down.

"Let me get this straight, you want me to put my foot on her stomach to make her think I'mma kick her in it, but stomp her somewhere else instead, then come back and stomp her stomach?" I nodded. "Damn yo' you a cold muthafucka'. What if she ain't fuckin' dude and it is yo' baby? My cousin for that matter?" I wasn't about to answer that, I knew Cola was bein' a lil' unfaithful slut.

"Tara, if you wanna make fifteen stacks, you ain't gon' worry about yo' so called cousin. I'm payin' yo' girls five stacks a piece. I'll text you when I'm ready for y'all."

I could tell she didn't want to do it by the look on her face. Money was the root of all evil. No job was too evil for Tara if the money was right. She loved money so much, she got a small dollar sign tattooed under her right eye. I left her sittin' there after I paid for our food.

On a Saturday night, Cola went to get some food. As soon as the door closed, I called Tara to tell her I wanted it done right now. I told Tara what Cola had on and what restaurant she was goin' to. I put Tara and four of her friends in a house a couple blocks away from the buildin' I lived in wit' Cola. The house belonged to a crackhead *named Bull. I gave him an eight ball to use his house for a couple weeks.*

I waited on Tara to call me after it was over, she came over instead. "What the fuck did you come over here for? What if she on her way back here to tell me what happened? You need to move around."

Tara pushed past me to come in the house. "I feel bad about this fam. She layin' out there bleedin' and shit." I smiled at the thought of that lil bastard baby seepin' all over the ground. "You smilin' 'bout this shit? You crazier than I thought."

My phone rang in the middle of my conversation wit' Tara. When I saw the name that popped up, I thought he was about to ask me about his blocks again. To my surprise he was calling to tell me about what happened to Cola.

"Y'all did good. I gotta go to the hospital to see about my girl. I'mma get up...." Before I could finish my sentence, Tara let her female side come out.

"I can't believe yo' bitch ass gon' go to that hospital

and act like you ain't set this shit up. This is exactly why I like pussy. Niggas is grimy. You foul as shit for this, Zell. I should go to that hospital and tell her you was behind it. I feel bad as hell for that girl."

I lifted her off of her feet by her neck. "Bitch, if I think you even havin' thoughts about tellin' anybody this shit, I will cut yo' tongue out yo' mouth and stick it up yo' ass." Lettin' her go, I walked to my closet, and grabbed the Nike duffle bag that held the $35,000 payment in it. I opened it up and watched as Tara's eyes lit up. "That mouth of yours cost you this. Get the fuck out my house."

"Payback is a bitch. You gon' get yours one way or another jo'." Tara walked out the door pissed off she didn't get her money. Fuck her, she shouldn't have come over here on that soft shit.

I called Kee while I was on my way to the hospital, she beat me there. I didn't feel guilty lookin' at Cola beat up like that. That shit had to be done. I wasn't about to take care of another nigga's baby unless it was there before me.

"How you feeling?" Kee asked as she put her hand on my knee and caressed it.

I had to put on a sad face. "I'm fucked up Kee, I didn't get to see what my child was gon' look like or how it was gon' be." Kee just sat there rubbin' my knee while I talked.

"I know, Zell. You have to help her get through this cause she gon' need you. Go check on her instead of sittin' out here, it's making Jay ask questions about whether you had a hand in this or not. It's important that you be there for her. She has me and Jay, but she wants you to be there. Get yourself together and be there for your girl."

"You right Kee. She lucky to have you as a friend." She smiled as she walked to the elevator. I shook my head at that nothin' ass bitch when she walked off. Kee ain't shit and she knew it.

As I was walkin' in Cola's room, Jay was walkin' out. He looked me dead in my eyes. "Where was you at?" I didn't answer him. "Nigga, if I find out you had anything to do wit' this I'mma kill yo' bitch ass. Yo' actions speaking volumes." He bumped shoulders wit' me. "Pussy ass nigga."

Jay didn't like me and he wasn't my favorite person either. We only respected each other on behalf of Cola. If it wasn't for her, one of us would have been dead a long time ago. Jay had a problem wit' me from the very beginning. I took it as him being a protective brother. The only problem I had wit' Jay was he was getting more money than I was.

Cola was sleep when I walked into the room. When she woke up, I asked her what I wanted to know. Cola was nice, but she was a pistol when she wanted to be. After she cursed me out, she told me what it was between her and Cash. I just sat there wit' no remorse until she put me out her room.

I left the room with my head held high feelin' like I accomplished somethin' major. I stopped at the nurse's station to find out any information on when they would release Cola, so I could be there to pick her up. I drove home in silence, only the thoughts in my mind could be heard by me.

Pullin' into my parkin' spot, I looked at the clock. It was four in the mornin'. Do these bitches ever sleep, I asked myself. Peachy and her girls were out drinkin' and listenin' to music comin' from an old beat up Saturn. I *parked in my spot, hopped out the car, nodded to them, and then walked to the buildin'.*

I felt a hand on my shoulder. "How Cola is?" Peachy was so close to me, I could smell the Hennessy on her breath.

"Not too good," I said as the elevator door opened. She got on the elevator with me.

"It's fucked up what had happened to her. I wish I woulda known it was her. I woulda helped her. How the baby is?" Whenever Peachy talked, I got a headache.

"She lost it." The elevator reached my floor, I stepped off and so did Peachy. I reached in my pocket for my keys with Peachy right behind me. "Aight Peachy, I'll holla at you later." I stepped halfway inside the door before she grabbed my arm.

"You 'ont want no company? You ain't gots to be by yo'self." She licked her lips.

Peachy was easy on the eyes. She made many niggas stop traffic, despite the many colors of weave she wore. Peachy had the potential to have any man she wanted, but she turned men off bein' so damn ghetto. To us she was good for one thing and one thing only.

"Oh shit! Aaahhh! Anybody ever told you that you suck dick like it's goin' out of style? Damn." Peachy's head game was superb. I tried to resist her, but her mouth was a lethal weapon. She put my dick and balls in her mouth at the same time and still had room to stuff an ice cube in her mouth. That ice drove me crazy. I felt myself about to explode. Unable to hold back, I shot my kids all over her face without warnin'.

"Yup, I been told that a lot." She picked my shirt up from the floor and wiped her face off wit' it.

"Damn…" I zipped my pants up. Peachy was getting' undressed. "What you doin'? You gotta go." I noticed Peachy was standin' there lookin' confused. "You just gon' stand there and look stupid or are you gon' get the fuck out?" She still just stood there. I walked over to her and pushed her towards the door.

I wasn't about to fuck Peachy. All she was good for was suckin' dick. That was the most I would ever do with her ass. I'd been gettin' dome from Peachy for a couple months. One night, while I was drunk, Peachy offered her mouth service. Cola was trippin' at the time, so I took Peachy up on her offer and it'd been goin' on ever since. She looked hurt when I said she had to go, I didn't give a fuck. As far as I was concerned her job was done.

Once she was outside my apartment she said, "For why we 'on't never fuck?" I looked at her like she was crazy. How can somebody so pretty talk so ugly?

"If you think I'mma fuck you, so you can run around and tell everybody, you dumber than I thought. You only get to suck my dick 'cause I know you ain't gon' let nobody know all you good for is dick sucking. I will never want you for nothin' more."

"How Cola would feel 'bout this?"

I snatched her back in the house by her purple, yellow, and blue weave. I didn't want Cola to find out I been messin' wit' somebody like Peachy. She was pretty and all, but she was Peachy. She was the stereotype that other races had about black people. Playin' like I cared, I got her a glass of water and made small talk.

"I thought that would change yo' mind. Now give me that dick."

"You want this dick?"

"Yup."

"How bad you want it?" I walked close to her and palmed her big ass.

"Real bad."

"Take it then."

She started unzipping my pants. Peachy was so focused on gettin' to my dick, she didn't notice me pull out my .45. She was givin' me slow head and givin' the tip of my dick soft kisses. I jumped back and pressed my gun against her left cheek.

Pop.

The bullet from my .45 went in one cheek and out the other. Peachy fell back in shock. A stream of tears fell down her face. I bet she'll think long and hard before she threaten me again.

"Bitches like you ain't never satisfied wit' what you got. You knew yo' place when we first started this shit, now you wanna fuck up my relationship. If I see you talkin' to Cola I'mma make sure I kill yo' ass. You understand?"

Fear and pain was all over her face when she bobbed her head up and down lettin' me know she understood me. I opened the door for her to leave, she ran full speed to the staircase holdin' both cheeks. A trail of blood was visible from my livin' room to the staircase. I wasn't worried about her tellin' anybody anything. I cleaned the blood up, then went to sleep like nothin' happened. That was the last time I saw Peachy for a long time.

Now that I think back on it, I was fucked up for fuckin' wit' Peachy. That's a'ight, though, I planned on making all that shit up to her now. She was my first love and I have a chance for a fresh start wit' her.

Cola

I snapped back to reality, still standing behind Zell. "Congrats," was the only word that escaped my mouth. We went our separate ways a while ago, he moved on and I wasn't mad at him for that.

"Shit, I don't even want the baby. I ain't in love wit' her, hell, I don't love her or even like her for that matter. She somebody I used to take my mind off you."

Getting rid of Anaya was going to be easier than I thought. "Well if you don't want to be with her you need to tell her that as soon as possible. It's not right to play with people's emotions. It could get you hurt."

"You right. What you on today? I gotta take care of some business early, but I wanna see you later. This shit crazy, you only been back for a day and all these old feelings are back."

"I have to go see Kee, we got a lot to talk about," I laughed. I knew Kee was going to have a million questions about how I ended up spending the night with Zell. "Yeah it's crazy, of all the I could've walked up to, it happened to be you. You got to figure out what you want to do with those feelings."

"I already know what I wanna do wit' 'em. You the only woman that made me weak. I thought about you every day. You was down for me and I was too dumb to see it. I want us to get back together Co."

"Talk to me when you take care of that situation with your girl. I'll be damned if I play the fool for you again." We went through hell and back with each other and at one point he owned my heart, however, he broke it a thousand times.

Zell dropped me off near Kee's house. I knew I was gon' hear it when I walked in the door. I really didn't wanna go in, but I didn't have a choice. I pulled out my phone to call Kee and let her know I was outside.

Kee opened the door with a glass of wine in her hand. My home girl loved her some wine. "Hey chick," I said as I plopped down on her couch. "I got some stuff to tell you."

Kee sipped her wine. "I'm listening." I explained everything to her from beginning to end. "He is so, just ugh, I have no words for him. I can't wait until he get what's coming to him for what he did to us. Especially you." I loved my friend, she was always there when I needed her. She was the most loyal, supportive, caring person I had ever met. "Wait did you let him drop you off here?"

"Hell no. I had him drop me off four blocks away."

"Alright."

As we sat around on talking, I started to think back on what happened with Kee that led us to where we are today…

Kee was the product of rape, but she never let that bother her. Her mother, Pam, was raped at the age of fifteen by two men. She found out she was pregnant two months later. Pam's mother wouldn't allow her to get an abortion, she told Pam children were a blessing in disguise.

On a hot June day, Keema Shanell Clark was born. Pam never really bonded with Kee, she acted as if she didn't exist. Pam had another daughter three years later who she adored. When Kee got old enough to understand things, she asked her mother, "Why don't you love me like you love Pooh mama?"

Pam turned to her 14-year-old daughter with hatred in her eyes. "I didn't want you. Those motherfuckers should have made me swallow you that night, then your ugly ass wouldn't be here."

Hurt, Kee ran six blocks to where I lived. After she told me what happened, I told my mother, Angie, what happened. My mother was fuming mad when she got up and left the house. When she returned, she had suitcases with her; she said Kee was staying with us. My mother raised Kee like her own. Kee never went back home after that day. I thought my mother was an angel. I missed her so much; she died of cancer a year ago.

Kee was short, light skinned with big bright brown eyes. She kept her hair cut short with a side bang that covered her eye. She was small, but her five foot two frame still had curves. My friend was beautiful inside and out.

"Where is Baker and Londyn, Kee?"

"I think they in the room. I heard the TV when I came in from work."

"Let me go back there and see them." Approaching the bedroom door, I smelled weed. Pissed off, I picked up my pace as I headed towards the room. "Baker, I know your monkey ass is not smoking around Londyn." I stopped dead in my tracks when I saw who was sitting there on the bed smoking a blunt. "What are you doing here?"

"Baker called me to come chop it up wit' him about you and Zell. He ain't happy about you spending the night wit' that fuck nigga."

"Jay, I didn't do anything with him. He slept on the floor while I was on the couch. I had to make things seem real. Where is Baker at anyway?"

"If he hurt you I'mma kill every single one of his family members, then I'mma dig them dead bitches up, and kill 'em again. That con artist Londyn wanted some ice cream. She suckered Baker into taking her."

"Nothing will happen to me, besides, I should win an Oscar for my acting skills. I had fake tears and everything. Zell believed everything I told him, he even tried to pretend like he felt bad about it."

"Fraud ass nigga." Jay stood up to put his shirt on. When he raised his arm, I saw the scar Zell caused when he stabbed Jay a couple days ago. Seeing his wounds caused me to have a flashback to what caused it…

The day I left Zell, he got shot. Word on the streets was he was saying Jay did it. That was semi true. Those two never liked each other. Jay didn't like Zell because of me and Zell didn't like Jay because he was getting a lot more money than he was. He wanted what Jay had so badly, he sent a boy named Feek to Jay to get put on one of his blocks.

After a few tests of loyalty, Jay set him up on a block.
Feek would swap Jay's product with some bad heroin Zell
gave him to sell on Jay's block. It was an attempt to run his
customers away. When Jay found out what was going on,
he followed Feek home one night.

Ready to kill, he put on the red and black Nike football
gloves he wore on what he called special occasions. Jay
picked the lock on the back door, walked through the
house, and checked all three bedrooms. An old woman
occupied one, a teenage girl was sleeping in another, and
Feek was in the third. Jay snatched him out of his bed and
put his gun directly to his temple.

Jay walked Feek to his sleeping grandmother's room.
He quietly walked beside her bed and placed the gun close
to her chest. Feek was scared to death. Jay raised his gun
to Feek and motioned him to his sister's room. Jay placed
the gun to her head. Feek's eyes began to water at the
sight in front of him.

Jay yanked Feek out of his sister's room by his shirt
and threw him against the wall. He spared Feek because

he was young. Jay did warn him that if he ever tried to play him again, he would make sure him, his grandmother, and sister were buried in the same grave. Feek assured Jay he wouldn't come near his block again. He didn't care if Feek came on the block; he only wanted to send a message about the importance of being loyal.

"I can't believe Zell stabbed you Jay," I said snapping out of my daze.

"That nigga dumb sis. He should have finished the job on his own instead of using some youngin's to do it."

"You think that girl you was with had anything to do with it?" I asked Jay, referring to the girl that was at his apartment earlier that night. Jay can be hardheaded at times. I told him numerous times to be careful when he came to the city. For the most part he did until he met some girl that ran her mouth like a faucet. Everybody knew where Jay was taking her and when. My guess was Zell heard about it and used that opportunity to try to kill Jay.

"Naw, she probably the reason he knew where I would be at because she talk too much. She ain't grimy enough to set me up. I talked to her after it happened and I could tell by the pitch in her voice that she didn't have nothin' to do wit' it. I'm done wit' her, though, she will have all my business in the streets if I keep fuckin' wit' her." He shook his head. "Why y'all women talk so much?"

"No, you always messing with them females that acts like they've never had a man with money. Step your game up and get a woman that's been there and done that. One that will act like that money you have is only chump change."

"Girl stop, I don't be serious about these broads."

"I guess."

"You better know it."

"Jay, Zell has a girlfriend. I been deleting her calls and shit just to make her back off for a few days. Eventually, she is going to call him again, she's pregnant. They have to communicate about that and I don't want her or her baby to get hurt, they're both innocent."

"Sis, I give you my word nobody innocent will get hurt. We want Zell and only Zell."

"Alright." I trusted Jay when he said she wouldn't get hurt. My mother raised Jay to never put his hands on a woman unless it was a matter of life and death.

Jay and I were born and raised in the Ickes projects on 23rd and State Street. That's were Jay fell in love with the drug dealing lifestyle. Our mother had to raise us by herself when our father got locked up before Jay was born. We never struggled because our father left enough money for us to be taken care of for a long time. Not to mention our mother had a good job working for the state. No matter how much money she had she wouldn't leave those buildings until she had no choice.

Jay and I had always been close. My mother told us if anything happened to her all we had was each other. We took that and ran with it. We had each other's back and covered for each other when we were doing stuff we didn't have any business doing.

I was the oldest, but Jay thought he was. He always sized up any boys that came to the house for me and I did the same thing with the girls he brought over. Jay always had different girls over and I wanted to make sure he was being safe. He moved from female to female so much I had to pray his dick wouldn't fall off.

By the time Jay was seventeen he was heavy in the streets thanks to an older guy named Meechi. Meechi had every young, old, fat, skinny, and ugly woman in the hood wanting him. He had his sights set on me ever since I was fifteen. I wouldn't give him the time of day even though I wanted to.

I would have gotten my ass whooped up and down State Street by my mother and Jay for messing with a man in his twenties. Meechi took Jay under his wing and showed him everything he needed to know about being a hustler. When Meechi got locked up, Jay got his money together and started his own operation.

When my mother moved out of the projects, Kee had just gotten her own apartment after finishing nursing school. Jay had a girl he actually liked named Marlene. He would be back and forth between his house and her house. As for me I was already living with Zell.

It was hard to believe he tried to kill my brother. This fool had the nerve to console me like he didn't have anything to do with it. He was really some kind of special, but payback was on the way.

Cola

"Mommy!!" I heard Londyn scream as I lay sleeping on the couch. "I got chicken and stwawbewwy ice cweam." Londyn couldn't pronounce words with the letter "r" in them, she made a "w" sound instead. She was three years old and the spitting image of me, only she had her father's complexion. My baby girl could talk a mile a minute. "Mommy, you sleepy? Can we go to the pawk?" I picked Londyn up to give her a kiss.

"Daddy can take you to the park later, go see your Uncle Jay. He said he was taking you to the toy store today." Those pretty bluish-gray eyes of hers lit up like a candle as she ran to the room Jay was in.

I could hear her all the way in the living room. "Uncle Jay, we going to get toys cause that's what mommy said." I knew Jay would take her wherever she wanted to go. She was his only niece. She had him wrapped around her finger.

"Bye mommy and daddy," Londyn said as her and Jay left the house. Jay shot me a death stare then smiled and shook his head.

"Bye baby, I'll see you later," Baker said bye to Londyn before she walked out of the door.

"Come here baby," I said to Baker.

"Fuck that. You spent the night with this nigga. When I agreed to let you do this, I told you to keep yo' phone on at all times." Baker was so pissed, his light skin turned red.

"You got a daughter to take care of and the only thing you supposed to be doing is finding out where this nigga rest his head at."

"My phone was on—"

Baker cut me off mid-sentence, "Cola I'm not about to sit here while another muthafucka parade around wit' you on his arm. If you gon' do this type of shit you need to be single and childless."

"What are you saying? You gon' leave me and take Londyn with you?" I usually didn't get mad at Baker, but he made me mad with that bullshit he said. He knew our little family meant the world to me. There was no way I would pick revenge over him and Londyn.

"That's exactly what I'm saying. If he finds out what you up to, what do you think is gon' happen? He already took a baby from you, do you think he'll think twice about killin' you? What if he finds out about Londyn, then what?" None of those things ever crossed my mind. Maybe Baker was right, maybe I should just let him and Jay handle things.

"I never thought about any of that. I love you and Londyn so much, I would die if anything happened to her because of me."

I looked into those bluish-gray eyes that were identical to our daughter's. Baker was definitely eye candy. My baby was six feet two with a muscular body. Baker wasn't all big and bulky with the muscles; he was cut just right.

He rocked a baldhead that was always shaved and soft. If he saw one hair on his head, you better know he would be in the bathroom shaving it. His beard was always lined and trimmed to perfection. His light complexion matched those eyes that I loved so much. I replayed the day I met him for the second time in my head...

It had been eight months since I lost the baby and I hadn't been anywhere because I was so depressed. All I did was think about my baby. Kee called me to go to this picnic with her. I didn't want to go because I still wasn't feeling social, plus, I knew Zell would be there.

We still didn't talk to each other too much. Kee practically begged me to come with her to the picnic at this park not too far from where I lived. I agreed after she assured me that I would have fun.

We made it to the picnic early, most people weren't there yet. Kee looked around like she was looking for somebody. When I felt her grab my arm, I knew she found who she was looking for. I looked at the group of men we were walking towards and only recognized Duke, Kee's boyfriend at the time. Kee walked up to Duke with her arms out for a hug.

"Hey, Coke-a-Cola," Duke said with his arms still around Kee. "You been hibernating on us."

"Hey Duke!" I loved Duke. He treated Kee like she deserved to be treated. I noticed the welcome home banners taped to the fence. "Whose picnic is this Duke?"

"This my man Baker picnic, he better show up. He don't like being in the spotlight."

Duke stopped talking and looked in the direction Kee was heading, I looked also. Zell was standing there with some video model looking chick. My blood was boiling inside. Kee's mouth and neck were moving in sync. I knew she was ripping Zell a new asshole for bringing that girl out in public.

Duke looked at me. "Cola, you need to leave dude's ass alone. He disrespectful and it's always been something about him that I don't like. Look at my Boo Boo giving him the business." We both looked as Kee went off.

"You right, Duke, I do need to let him go. I'm tired of him cheating and disrespecting me."

"I don't want your heart to keep gettin' broke. This nigga ain't right for you."

Duke was like another brother to me, may he rest in peace. For the short period of time Duke was around, he looked out for me just as much as Jay did.

As I was about to walk over to Zell, Duke grabbed me to introduce me to the man of the hour.

Without looking at me he said, "What up doe?" Then said to Duke, "Yo' girl over there giving it to Zell's bitch ass." They both laughed.

So this is Baker, I thought to myself. The last time I saw him was eight months ago. I was so bruised and bloody he probably didn't remember me, but I remembered him. Those eyes were unforgettable.

"Cola, can you believe that son of a bitch brought that hoe out here like she his girl. I hate that jackass," Kee yelled breaking me out of my daze. "I'm sorry Cola, but he's too damn disrespectful. You over here and he out there with some two dollar hoe."

"You have no reason to be sorry, Kee. He gon' get what's coming to him in due time." Kee gave me a hug before she went to talk to Duke. I walked over to the table where the drinks were being served. A few shots of Patron would be nice right about now.

"Can I talk to you for a minute?" Zell stood behind me along with the chick he came with. I looked down and this nigga was holding her hand. Zell must've been feeling good that day because he was really taking it there. I ignored him while I got my shot. "What you doin' outside? You need to go home."

"Hold on, nigga you got me fucked up if you think you about to stand in my face talking to me while you holding another bitch's hand. I been nothing but good to you, yet *you always doing something to hurt me. I lost the baby months ago, not once did you ask me if I was okay or if I needed anything. You didn't even comfort me when I cried. Now you concerned about me because I messed up your flow? Fuck you and everything you stand for, Bitch."*

The girl had a smirk on her face. This bitch must've thought I was a joke. Let's see if she still had a smirk after this. I grabbed a bottle of Goose off the table, broke the bottle on the table, and then slashed her face and Zell's shoulder. They never saw it coming.

"AHHHHHH!! MY FACE! MY FACE!" she screamed while holding her face.

"You should have been worried about your face when you had that stupid ass smirk on it. Now, I would advise you to get the fuck away from me before this bottle be sticking out that long ass neck of yours." She ran out of the park like a bat out of hell.

"I'm about to beat yo' ass out here!" Zell said while holding his bloody shoulder.

"You not about to do shit to me unless you don't like

your life. Jay been wanting to handle you for the longest. Try to put your hands on me if you want to, I bet today will be the last day you walk this Earth."

I didn't cut him deep enough to cause any damage. Truth is, I didn't want to hurt him bad at all, I was just fed up. I didn't know what came over me that day; I was totally out of character. Zell deserved what he got. He left the park bloody and mad.

It didn't surprise me that nobody tried to stop what happened, not too many people liked him. He was a savage. A couple people asked me was I okay after what happened, I assured them I was cool. The picnic resumed like nothing happened.

"Don't cut me," I heard a deep voice say from behind me. I turned around to face Baker. "I thought you was gon' kill him."

"Scare him, yes. Kill him, no. All he has is a scratch, it was time for him to learn a lesson." I looked over at Baker trying to read his expression.

"The last time I saw you, you were in bad shape. How

are you doing?"

My mind was all over the place. Standing in front of me was the man that called the ambulance for me and stayed with me until they came. He asked me a question Zell hadn't asked me at all.

"I'm holding up. I lost my baby, but I'm slowly getting over that. How do you know Zell?"

"I'm sorry about the baby. I always wondered what happened to you after that night. Zell used to work for me before I got locked up. I let him run things temporarily while I was gone. Somehow he managed to fuck things up."

"You just told me your business, you trust me already? What if I was the FEDS?" I batted my eyelashes to let him know I was flirting.

"Call me crazy, but I do trust you. I think you just as crazy, though. Anybody that will cut two muthafuckas in the middle of a crowded picnic ain't all the way there and they definitely ain't the FEDS."

"You can't call that crazy. That's called a woman

being fed up." I truly was fed up with Zell.

"Since you fed up you should let me take you out. I wanna show you what you worth. Me and Zell don't fuck wit' each other, so don't even give me that excuse. He did some foul shit that has made him my enemy. All respect was lost." He licked those juicy lips of his. That and the fact that I wanted to hurt Zell was enough to convince me to go out with him.

Things with Baker started out as just something to do to get back at Zell. As time passed, we developed feelings for each other. Baker was different from any man I'd ever been with. He was a gentleman at all times. He opened car doors, pulled out chairs, and ordered for me at restaurants. Sex wasn't an issue. Baker wouldn't have sex with me because I was still with Zell. He truly only wanted to show me my worth.

I didn't want Baker to be the reason I left Zell. I was always told to never leave the one you love for the one you like. Even though Zell was a jackass, for some dumb ass reason that was unknown to me, I held on to the love I once felt for him. That was why it was hard to leave him.

He wasn't always cold, sometimes he was the nicest man in the world.

Over the course of six months, I spent most of my time with Baker. Zell was so into his street business that he didn't notice I wasn't home as much. I started not to care who saw me with Baker. I would even let him drop me off at the apartment I shared with Zell. One night when Baker dropped me off, it turned out to be the best night of my life.

Baker and I went to a basketball game one night. After it was over, he dropped me off at home. I kissed him and told him to let me know when he made it home. I was falling out of love with Zell and falling in love with Baker. I walked inside the house still on cloud nine from my day with Baker. That mood quickly changed when I opened my bedroom door.

The sight I saw was too much for me. Zell and some girl were sleeping naked in my bed. I called Baker to come back and get me. The sex must have been good because they never moved while I packed my clothes. I contemplated bashing both of their heads in, but when I went to get the hammer, Baker was calling to tell me he was outside. I dropped the hammer, got my bags and left.

That same night Zell got shot while he was sleep. I felt like that was my fault because I didn't lock the door when I left. I tried to go back, but Baker wasn't having it.

Zell was trying to contact me from the hospital. I got so tired of seeing his name pop up on my screen that I asked Baker to get me a new phone. I didn't want the phone Zell bought me, nor did I want him to have my number. Kee let me stay with her for a while, I didn't want to rush things by living with Baker too soon.

Six months later, I got the news that I was two and a half months pregnant by Baker. He insisted that I move in with him. I wanted to live with Baker, but he lived in boring ass DeKalb, but eventually he convinced me to move an hour away from the city.

I didn't know at the time that he talked Kee and Jay into moving down there, too. It took me a few weeks to adjust to the quietness. I was used to always hearing somebody yelling, fighting, or shooting. Once I got used to not hearing the noise of the city, I actually liked DeKalb.

Seven months later, I gave birth to a precious baby girl who decided to make her debut in the world a couple of weeks late. I told my mother she could name her since she didn't get to use her name for the first baby. She loved Baker like a son and wanted him to be part of it. They decided to name her, Londyn Jaylah Wallace, giving her Baker's last name. Baker said my last name would be Wallace as well, so I shut up and didn't object to Londyn having his last name at all.

Life was good. I had a daughter who I adored and a man who took care of me, made sure I didn't want for anything, loved me unconditionally, and most of all he respected me. I was happy I decided to give Baker a chance. He was cut from a different cloth and I couldn't ask for a better man than him.

Jay and Baker went to the city every day to check on things, like they had real jobs. They left out early in the morning and came back late at night. Baker came home early at least three nights a week to avoid me nagging him. Baker went out with Zell's cousin Tara one night and I assumed Zell did her wrong in some kind of way because *she was telling Baker stuff he didn't know about Zell. Three incidents she spoke of held Baker's attention. Those three things and Zell trying to kill Jay were the reasons we were back in the city right now.*

"Cola," I heard Baker call out to me as I snapped back to reality. "I know he hurt you and old feelings may be resurfacing, but you gon' fuck yo' relationship up doing shit like this. You got the address where he lay his head at now let me take it from here."

"That's not where he lives. Where we were at last night is just somewhere he go every blue moon to chill." Baker didn't look happy. I knew he wanted me away from Zell. "Think about all the things Tara told you that night. The things that brought us back to the city. I want to hurry up and get this over with, too. I can't stand looking at him for too much longer."

"I told you I was gon' always keep you safe. If somethin' happens to you on account of him, shit gon' get real ugly." I kissed those soft lips of his.

"Nothing will to happen to me," I assured Baker. We stood in the middle of the room hugging each other like we had not seen each other in years.

"I love yo' ass. Straight up," he whispered in my ear.

"I love you, too, baby."

"I'm never letting you go. I would be a damn fool if I did."

"Awwwww, I just love black love," Kee said when she came in holding grocery bags. "You all…" she faked sniffled, "…are sooooo cute." She wiped a fake tear, we all laughed.

"I can't stand you, Kee," I said as she walked to the kitchen.

"I'm about to go take care of some business, be here when I get back, Cola."

"I'll be here." I went inside the pocket of his jeans; pulled out the wad of money he kept, peeled off six hundred dollar bills, and put the rest back in his pocket. Baker shook his head at me. "What? I want to go shopping today," I said with a smile on my face.

"You gon' take all my money."

"No, I'm not, I only want half."

He laughed and shook his head as he headed towards the door. I watched him as he got in his white Range Rover. I couldn't help but think about how much I loved that man.

Baker

"What up doe?"

"Shit. What you on? It ain't time to shut down, what you doin' over here, Baker?"

"I needed to holla at you, get in." Tara got in no

questions asked. "You heard anything from yo' cousin?" I had to pay Tara a visit just to see where Zell's head was at. I asked her to get back in tune wit' him to feel him out when Cola came back around.

"Yeah fam. He just called me earlier talkin' 'bout he getting' back together wit' Cola and he gon' treat her right this time. He said he gon' leave his pregnant girl for her."

I can understand why he was still in love with Cola. She was a good woman. I would probably be the same way if I lost her. My uncle used to always tell me, one man's trash is another man's treasure. Cola was definitely a treasure. Zell was too stupid to realize what he had.

"Back together?" I laughed. "What's his girl's name?"

"Anaya."

"What she look like?"

"Hell if I know, he never brought her around. From what he say, she a bad chocolate bitch, but she real stuck on herself." Tara took a puff of her blunt. "Shit I wanna see what she look like, I might take her." She was serious, Tara was known to turn straight women gay.

"Don't you got yo' hands full with the girl you got? Her ass seem like a handful." Suddenly her face became full of every different emotion I could think of. "You cool?"

"Nah fam. She was fuckin' wit' some nigga…" she looked down at the dirt covered ground that used to be grass, "…and she got AIDS jo'."

"You bullshittin'." I wasn't expecting that bomb to be dropped.

"I be keepin' my distance, not because I want to, she be on some other shit. Treatin' me like I'm the one that gave it to her. I wanna be there for her every step of the way, but she just won't let me." No matter how much of a man she acted and dressed like, Tara was still a woman. It was evident by the water forming in her eyes.

I hadn't seen Tara in some months. I automatically assumed she was still with Peachy. They'd been together for a long time. Tara knew she didn't like boys when she was fifteen. Peachy was seventeen when she noticed Tara looking at her like all the boys did. They ended up experimenting with each other, it turned out to be a very long project. They did the break up to make up thing. Somehow they always ended up back together, even after Tara found out about Peachy and Zell, she left her for a couple months, but like always, she went back.

I was trying to get in touch with Tara as soon as I got out. She was never home and the number I had on her was disconnected. Peachy happened to be out the same night I saw Cola getting jumped on. Peachy gave me Tara's number, I called her, but she never answered. I didn't know at the time that she was one of the girls that caused Cola to lose her baby.

Tara actually looked like a girl that night. Her hair wasn't in braids, it was curly and fell down to the middle of her back. She even had on women's clothes. I didn't recognize her at all, I don't think anybody did. The only thing that would have gave her away was the tattoo under her eye. Being smart, she covered it with makeup.

That same night Zell shot Peachy, she had no choice but to tell Tara everything. Tara fell off the face of the earth for a few months. She finally answered her phone for me a few weeks after the picnic Duke had for me. We met up at a bar a couple days later…

"My nigga, Baker," Tara said as she sat on the barstool.

"What up wit' yo' fuckin' cousin?" I got right to it. She was his cousin and I didn't know where they stood.

"I don't have a cousin."

"What happened?"

Tara sung like a bird, the more she talked the more shots I bought her. She told me how Zell shot her girl, the time he tried to shut Jay's blocks down by using Feek, how he never paid her and her girls to make sure Cola lost her baby, and how he choked her after she went to tell him what happened with Cola. That shit wasn't right. She also told me that it was Zell that set me up, the night I got locked up, and he was the one who killed Duke.

"I should have listened to Duke about fuckin' wit' Zell. What made him set me up, kill Duke, and do Cola like that?" I already knew why he tried to get down on Jay. I wanted to know about me, Cola, and Duke.

"He thought Cola was fuckin' wit' some nigga named Cash

who is the front man for this bar we sittin' in. The nigga that own this bar is Cola's brother. Jay used to have Cola drop off the money to Cash every Friday. Zell saw her one night, next thing I know he was givin' me exact instructions on how he wanted it done."

"He did her dirty. Did she lose the baby?" Seeing as how Cola was my girl now I already knew she lost the baby. I couldn't let Tara know any of that yet.

Tara's eyes began to water. "Yeah, she lost it. I feel bad 'bout that shit. It still eats me up at times." Honestly, I was thinking about killin' her ass right there for putting Co through that shit. The sincerity in her eyes made me think twice.

"Damn. I know you feel bad, but you gotta keep it movin'. Everybody makes mistakes in life, it's how you bounce back from them."

"True. I asked God to forgive me a thousand times."

"That's what's up. Now what about him setting me up? Why he do that?"

"He always been jealous of you, Baker. You always had the baddest bitches, nicest cars, money out the ass, and loyal niggas.

You didn't stand on the corner as long as he did. He used to always say, 'That pretty ass nigga never got his hands dirty. I'm out here riskin' my life and freedom droppin' this shit off while he somewhere fuckin' some bad bitch or worry free knowin' them people ain't gon' slide on him at any givin' moment'."

"Man that nigga had money and his girl was bad. I stood on the block just like every other nigga did. It ain't my fault I never let bitches and personal shit get in the way of me going to the top. Yeah, he risked his freedom and he got compensated nicely for that shit. He ain't have loyalty around him 'cause he ain't a loyal nigga, bottom line."

"I feel you." She took another shot of Patron. "Let me ask you somethin', do you think that nigga was sick that day you had to make the drop offs? Remember you couldn't find Skeet either?" I remember that day like it was yesterday. Skeet was the young boy I used to make drop offs when Zell couldn't or just from time to time to put some money in his pockets. "He told Skeet you wanted them to go to Maywood to pick somethin' up. He pulled up in front of a house, told Skeet to go around to the backdoor and knock three times. Skeet got out, leavin' his phone in the car, he took three steps and Zell pulled off. He left Skeet

stuck wit' no phone and no way to get back."

"Get the fuck outta here," I said not wanting to believe what she was saying.

"Dead ass fam. He called you that day to check on things, he just wanted to know what block you was droppin' off at next, so he could have the police waitin' on you. As soon as he hung up wit' you, he told the police where you was gon' make the drop off at, told them what kind of car you was in, and that you had a gun under the seat."

I couldn't believe that nigga set me up, lucky for me the first officer on the scene was Officer Carla Wallace, my favorite aunt. She knew what I was into in the streets. She searched my car, made the dope disappear, and took the clip out of my pistol before her partner walked up. He walked up as she was about to put the gun back under the seat. It wasn't loaded and it was registered to me, so I was good on that. When they ran my name, a warrant popped up from a year ago for some bullshit. I ended up doing six months.

I wanted Duke to run things while I was gone, but he went legit a few months before I got locked up, I wasn't gon' ask him to dive back in the game. My cousin was out west doing his own thing and my right hand man, Jake, had his hands full wit' the low end. Damn near everything from State to the Lake was Jake's responsibility. My homie Goo took over most of my blocks and I took a chance letting Zell take over the few blocks I had out east. I only had four blocks out there to put in work, it was easy to manage that, but Zell managed to fuck everything up in six months' time.

"What Duke have to do with anything?"

"Right after you got out, yo' auntie came through lookin' for Duke. Seein' as how she couldn't be seen socializin' wit' her drug kingpin nephew." I laughed at that statement and sipped on my Corona. "She finally caught up to Duke a week after yo' picnic. Turns out Zell would give her partner information from time to time. He didn't tell y'all he got pulled over wit' two bricks one day. That's the day he made a deal wit' the devil." Tara looked over at some female that was giving her the eye. "I'll be right back, I gotta have her." Tara was pissy drunk. She had to be, not to notice that woman looked like the character, Wanda, from 'In Living Color'. All I could do was laugh as Tara walked back over to me smiling from ear to ear. "I'mma fuck the shit outta that bitch tonight. My nigga do you see her?"

"Do you see her?" That woman was busted, her wig was twisted; she was cross-eyed and cockeyed. I didn't even know that shit was possible. She had on a pink pleather skirt, a blue tank top with a bleach stain on it and some brown heels that look like she had walked to hell and back in them. I shook my head when Tara made her way back over to me. "Back to Duke, though, what happened after my auntie saw him?"

"She let him know Zell was the one that snitched and Duke approached Zell about it. You know that nigga denied it like he was on trial for murder. Duke told Zell he was gon' see him. Zell got to Duke before he got to you, most importantly before Duke got to him." I ordered Tara her last shot of Patron. "Zell knew exactly what time Duke was gon' open his store up that next mornin'. He waited around the corner for him to pull up. When Duke was unlockin' the door, Zell crept up behind him and shot him up. He even took the nigga wallet and cell phone to make it look like he got robbed."

"Damn." Duke got shot seven times, three in the head alone, once in the back, twice in the arm and once in the leg. He was a good dude. I was fucked up when that shit happened. Duke was like my brother. He didn't have any enemies that I knew of. We really thought it was a robbery. My mans had to have a closed casket funeral because of Zell. "Why you ain't tell me none of this when it was goin' on?"

"Bitch ass nigga or not, he was still my cousin. When he played me, I stopped bein' loyal." I couldn't be mad at Tara for having loyalty to her family.

"Can't be mad at that. I got a couple blocks for you. I'mma hit you up once I set it all up." I slid her five stacks for the info she gave me. I wasn't expecting her to tell me the things she was telling me. She told me she would call me and walked to the end of the bar where that Wanda looking lady was sitting at.

As I was leaving, I bumped into Jay, "What up doe?"

"What's good wit' it? What you doing in my establishment? My sister know you outside?" Jay always had a joke about me and Cola. He told me I was pussy whipped. I was in love and didn't give a fuck who knew!

"My baby know every move I make." That statement was true. Cola knew I was going to meet up wit' Tara.

"I thought you was a real nigga, Baker," Jay joked.

"You should be glad yo' sister got a nigga like me." His face turned from playful to serious.

"You know I just be fuckin' wit' you. I'm happy she got a man like you. You make her happy. I can tell y'all really love each other. I've been protecting Cola from niggas ever since she got a shape to her. It feels good not to worry about somebody breaking her heart." Jay was the younger brother that acted like the older brother. He was only two years younger than Cola, but he acted like he was ten years older than she was.

"You on yo' period or somethin'? You sound real soft right now," I laughed.

"I did just sound like a bitch."

"You know Cola my heart and you don't have to worry about her." I meant that from the bottom of my heart. "Aye, you got an office in here? I need to holla at you for a minute."

"Follow me." We walked towards the back of the bar, Jay turned his head towards Tara and the Wanda look-a-like. "Maaann you gots to be shittin' me. Do you see that shit? She cock eyed and crossed eyed. Is that possible?" Unable to hold my laughter in, I held my stomach at the facial expression Jay had *on his face.*

We sat in the office for about twenty minutes while I explained everything Tara had just told me to Jay. Jay was so hot, he was about to put some lead in Tara right there in the middle of his bar. After I calmed him down, we talked.

"I'm seeing red right now, Baker. Where this muthafucka live at?"

"Remember when you put that chick on him?"

"Don't remind me."

"Exactly! We need to carefully plan somethin' for him. Last time you rushed it, shit didn't play out the way it should have."

The night Cola left Zell, she didn't know Jay planned somethin' as payback for sending Feek to him. I knew about it and I was all for it. Jay had this female named Marlene he used to mess with heavy. Jay told her he wanted her to shoot him directly in the heart. Marlene agreed to do it if Jay took her on a trip to Jamaica. He told her after it was done, they would be on a plane.

Marlene sold Zell a story of her visiting Chicago from

Atlanta. She told him she was sharing a hotel room with two other girls, so they couldn't go to her hotel room. She convinced Zell to take her to his apartment, the one he and Cola shared. Marlene was about to carry the deed out when she heard Cola come in. She played sleep until Cola left.

After Cola left, she crept past a still sleeping Zell to get dressed. She pulled out the pistol Jay gave her, hurried to the bed and pulled the trigger hitting Zell directly in the chest. Had she shot a few inches to the left she would have hit the exact location she was supposed to hit.

Marlene called Jay as soon as she was done to tell him she did it. A man of his word, he took her to Jamaica. Things went south when I called to tell him Zell survived. Jay put Marlene out of their hotel room. She slept outside the door that night since her wallet was in the room with Jay. The next day, Jay felt bad about what he did to her, so while they were still in Jamaica, he took her on a shopping spree. Developing amnesia regarding what Jay did to her, they were back to normal after that.

"So, you gon' tell Cola?"

"Not right now and you not either. Give me yo' word?" One thing about Jay was if he gave you his word, he kept it.

"When you plan on telling her?"

"Soon. Do I have yo' word you not gon' mention this to her?"

Jay let out a heavy sigh. "You got it. Tell her soon though, Baker."

"Both of us will tell her when the time is right."

"I'm wit' it," he said as he sat there in deep thought. I could tell Jay's trigger finger was itchin' by the look in his eyes.

"I'm gone, I gotta go get yo' spoiled ass sister some hot wings."

Jay laughed and said, "Aight lil errand boy."

"Fuck you bruh. I'll holla at you in the a.m."

"Aight."

Leaving Jay's office, I noticed Tara and "Wanda" were gone. I chuckled at the thought of what Tara's reaction would be when she saw what that woman really looked like. I got Cola her hot wings and turned in for the night.

Months had passed since I met up wit' Tara. When I finally

decided to tell Cola, as well as, Kee about everything, I didn't know how she was gon' take it. Jay and me discussed whether or not to tell her the role we had in her leaving Zell that night. We decided to put everything on the table.

Later that night we all sat in Kee's kitchen and I told them what I knew. Everybody was silent, Kee broke into tears when I told her what Zell did to Duke and Cola was trying to be strong. She didn't let any emotion show as I explained that it was Zell who set her up that night and that Jay and me was the reason she left Zell. Jay sat still and angry as he watched the two women he loved hurting.

I thought Cola was gon' go off on me after finding out that, in a way, we betrayed her. To my surprise Cola thanked us for doing that. She said if it wasn't for that night she would probably still be sleeping wit' the enemy.

Cola had a secret of her own to share. She revealed that she was pregnant wit' my first child. Kee's sad tears turned into happy tears. Jay actually had a full blown smile on his face, somethin' I never really saw on his face. I sat there in shock, I wasn't ready for kids, but at the same time, I was ready for anything with Cola.

She pulled me to the side as Kee talked baby talk to Jay who was looking at her like she was crazy. I asked if she was gon' keep it, she said yes. That was the end of the discussion.

In a few short months, I became the father to a beautiful baby girl. Londyn was the perfect mixture of us. She became the reason I lived. All four of us were so in love with Londyn, we never really spoke about Zell again.

Everything Tara told me resurfaced after Zell tried to kill Jay. We came back ready to paint the city red wit' Zell's blood. If he would have stayed low we wouldn't be at his ass. Zell got some shit started and you better believe we were gon' finish it.

Zell

After droppin' Cola off at her girl house, I went to holla at Feek and his man Spook. Them niggas really came through on that hit. Ever since I heard through the grapevine that Jay shot me a few years back, I wanted him so bad I could taste it. I searched high and low for him, as well as, Cola. I wanted to retaliate on him and win her heart back. Eventually, Jay resurfaced and I made my move as soon as I heard he was back.

"Feek and Spook, y'all pulled that off for a nigga." Spook looked at Feek confused. "She came runnin' to me tellin' me she found him exactly the way I told you to kill him."

"Can we get our money for that, I gotta get my son some pampers and milk," Feek said, Spook never said a word. His eyes shifted from person to person. Whoever was talkin' was who he looked at.

"Oh, y'all most definitely can get paid right now. I've been wantin' that done for a long time now." I pulled two white envelopes out of my back pocket. Both envelopes held what they thought was ten thousand dollars. Hope them lil niggas didn't know the difference between real and counterfeit money. Feek stuffed the envelope in his pocket. Spook did the same with his. "I gotta go holla at my soon to be ex, y'all good on the work?" Feek nodded his head. "Why you so quiet lil' nigga?"

"We good on the work, just thinkin' about my granny and sister," Feek said.

"I'm out."

Feek shot me a death stare. I brushed it off and kept walkin'
towards my car. I noticed Spook and Feek talkin' as I pulled off.
I found it odd that they were so quiet. You would think they
would be happy about being twenty thousand dollars richer. To
be honest they were only a few hundred dollars richer. They
probably won't realize it until they get locked up for spending
fake money.

Feek

"Yo' Feek you think he gon' come lookin' for us when he find out we sold him out to Jay?" Spook asked.

"We gon' be long gone by the time he get that news. Besides, Jay paid us a hundred thousand for lettin' him know what was up. I don't know about you, but I'm packin' my family up and leavin' right now. You can come if you want to. We can take over somebody city with the money we got from Jay and Zell."

Spook and Feek had been friends ever since they were in preschool. Feek didn't mind Spook tagging along with them,

Spook didn't have any family. He had lived with Feek's family since he was 8 years old. Spook was born to a drug addicted mother and father, who only cared about getting high. Spook was on the verge of being homeless because his mother couldn't afford the $50 low income rent she had in the projects. Feek's grandmother let him sleep in the basement from that point on.

Feek never admitted it to Spook, but he secretly admired Jay's style. He actually wanted to be like him. A man with money, power, respect, loyalty, fear, and women. Everybody loved Jay and if you didn't love him you feared him.

Feek knew he couldn't blame anybody, but himself for almost costing his family their lives. It's a dirty game in the streets of Chicago. He knew the risk he was taking when Zell approached him about selling bad heroin on Jay's block. Needing money, he took Zell up on his offer.

Feek told his grandmother about what happened. He felt like it was the right thing to do. She packed up and took his sister to Memphis, Tennessee. She was mad at Feek for bringing trouble to her doorstep, but she loved him for telling her about it. She always told Feek when he moved out she would move back down south. Feek took what happened as a sign to let his grandmother go to her place of birth earlier than expected. Feek wouldn't go, he didn't like Memphis.

"Feek, you the only family I got now."

"Come on then, we gone."

Feek and Spook got in Spook's brand new to Spook, but used Grand Prix and left the block to run itself. When they pulled off, they never looked back. Feek called his girlfriend, told her to pack them some clothes and be downstairs in thirty minutes.

Like clockwork as they were pulling up, Feek's girl was coming out struggling with bags of clothes and their son running around the curb. They stopped at Wal-Mart to get the baby a car seat for the long drive and some snacks, then they went to the nearest gas station to fill the car up.

"Where we goin' Feek?" Spook asked as he pumped gas.

It didn't take long for Feek to answer, "Miami."

Spook smiled thinking of the women and the weather. Feek texted the number Jay gave him to tell him they were gone.

Zell

It seemed strange that Anaya hadn't called me since our fight. Usually, she called within two days. It'd been three days since I left the house. None of the lights were on in the house. Thank God she wasn't home. I was gonna pack some clothes and leave.

Steppin' inside the door, I almost tripped over a pair of wheat Timberland boots. She didn't wear gym shoes or Timbs, so I knew she had a nigga in here. I crept up the stairs, I heard

Anaya's soft moans and a different voice. The other voice belonged to another woman. I knew she was into women; that was one of the reasons we lasted this long. Those threesomes we had kept me there.

I opened the bedroom door to find Anaya's legs in the air, eyes closed, and mouth wide open from the head this woman, wit' the biggest ass I have ever seen, was givin' her. I didn't care what her face looked like, that ass was right. Anaya opened her eyes and noticed me standin' in the doorway. Wit' her finger she motioned for me to come to her. I came home to leave her and pack some clothes, but the sight before me clouded my judgment.

Before I knew it, Anaya unzipped my pants. When I bent down to kiss her she whispered in my ear, "I want to look at you while you hitting her from the back."

Shit she didn't have to tell me twice. I wasted no time doin' what she wanted me to do. This woman had the tightest wettest pussy I had ever felt. Anaya got head the whole time while she looked at me give her female friend the business from the back. This woman was moanin' like no tomorrow.

Finally, I let go all over her ass, as she made Anaya cum for what seemed like the hundredth time. When Anaya's legs stopped shakin', the girl between them started to rise up, her body was bangin'. She turned around to face me.

"Peachy? What the fuck?"

"Zell? Wow, that was better than I thought it woulda been," she said with an evil grin on her face. I noticed those man made dimples I gave her. They actually looked good, like they were supposed to be there.

"Who you tellin'? How y'all end up together?"

Curiosity as well as regret were consumin' me. I wanted to know how they ended up together and I regretted fuckin' Peachy. It was good, but it was Peachy. She couldn't decide if she was gay or straight from one day to the next. She upgraded herself since I last saw her. She didn't have five bright colors of weave in her hair or those eight inch nails she usually had. She had a jet black weave with Chinese bangs and a French manicure on her fingers and toes.

"I had met her last night at the corner sto'," Peachy said.

"You two know each other?" Anaya asked.

"Yeah we used to know each other," I said as I took in the

two naked women layin' on the bed. Peachy kept this devious smile on her face, I couldn't help but wonder what that was about.

"You should have kept her around and brought her home sometimes. It's time for round two," Anaya said as she winked at Peachy, who still had a wicked smile on her face.

Anaya flipped Peachy on her back and placed her head between her legs. This time it was Anaya's turn to get pleased by me. Every now and then I glanced at Peachy, that wicked smile was still there every time I looked. I ignored it and kept fuckin' Anaya. We had fun for hours, but all good things must come to an end. Peachy left and Anaya wanted to talk.

"What you wanna talk about?"

"I wanted to tell you how sorry I am for what I said to you the other day, I didn't mean that. Being pregnant has my hormones all over the place." Here she go usin' pregnancy as an excuse for bein' selfish and stupid. "I love you Zell, we're about to have a baby. I want our relationship to last." I couldn't deny that I did treat her bad at times. She so stuck up it was ridiculous. Sometimes I had to get her up off that high horse.

"Naya, you too damn stuck on yo'self for me. If I take you out the only thing you worried about is if yo' outfit cost more than the next bitch or if yo' weave is more expensive. I don't like yo' ass."

"I will not step out this house looking nothing less than great. I refuse to look like them busted girls from the projects. My weave alone cost more than what those broke bitches pay for their rent. Do you see this face and body? I have every right to be stuck on this." She just named every reason why I didn't like her. I shook my head at everything she just said.

"Naya, you dumb."

"How am I dumb because I know I look good? If a man wants me he's going to have to keep me up, including you. You been doing it, why all of a sudden you complaining about it now?"

"Because I'm leavin' yo' cute ass for somebody that's the exact opposite of you. Yo' problem is you think the world owe you somethin' because you look good. When you take all that make up off you ain't even cute."

"Negro please I'm the hottest thing you have ever had. Cola

is the only girl you had that comes close to looking as good as me. Muthafucka said I ain't hot." Her weave was swingin' from left to right while she went off. "And from the picture I saw, that bitch body don't compare to this." She traced her body with her hands from her breasts to her thighs.

"Watch yo' fuckin' mouth about her."

"Oh, wow. Why you defending that red head bitch? Is that who you leaving me for? The same bitch that didn't come to the hospital to see ya' half dead ass?" She was really goin' there.

"Bitch, didn't I tell you to watch yo' mouth and that's exactly who I'm leavin' you for."

"But you call me dumb? I hope y'all have fun with each other."

"We will definitely have fun. I'mma give her whatever she want, we gon' have a baby, come take yo' baby and raise it like it's ours." I was serious, I had my life with Cola planned out already. I'mma do whatever I gotta do to make it work this time.

"HAHAHAHA!!! You should be a comedian. You sound like a little ass boy right now."

"You know I don't want that baby right? And I want a DNA test," I said as I packed my clothes.

"Who cares what you want? Just keep the same number. As soon as I pop this baby out we can take the test."

"Cool."

While I was packin' my clothes, my phone alerted me that I had a text message. It was from Cola.

Hey I can't make it tonight I have to take a rain check I'll call you in a couple days xoxo

I guess the disappointment was all over my face because Naya had somethin' to say.

"Uh oh, you got the shit face. Got cancelled on, huh? She probably with her real man," Anaya laughed.

"Would you shut up?"

I wondered what Cola was gon' be doin' for the next couple of days that I wouldn't be able to see her. I guess I'll get my apartment on Lake Shore Drive furnished. I plan on moving Cola in soon. I knew I was rushin' things, but she been gone for too long, I didn't want to waste any more time.

Cola

After Baker left, I dragged Kee to the mall with me. I wanted to go get something to wear for Baker tonight. I loved that he was simple and didn't like all the fancy lace shit. He was cool with me being in a t-shirt and a pair of bikini panties, especially some black ones. After we left there, I saw some limited edition Bo Jackson's in Footlocker that I had to have. I got Baker and I a pair, they didn't have my baby girl's size. She ended up with a pair of pink Chucks.

Kee and I went to a few more stores. All those high end expensive clothes weren't really my style. I wore name brand stuff sometimes. For the most part, I was simple. That's one of the things Baker said he loved about me, my simplicity.

After we finished shopping, we sat at the food court and ate. I always had a good time with Kee. She was always honest and gave great advice.

"Kee, you worried about me doing this?"

"Yes. Not because I don't think you can't handle it, it's because Zell a little off, Co. I'm worried about if his cousin is going to tell him."

"I don't think she will, from what Baker tells me as long as he paying her nice to run a couple blocks for him and giving her an occasional bonus for telling him everything Zell did, she will be loyal to him. Plus she scared of him and Jay."

"Name a person that's not scared of Jay." We both laughed.

Jay was really sweet once you got past that tough outer layer. We resembled each other a lot. We were the exact same height, he was a shade lighter than me. We had the same slanted eyes, only his didn't hold pain like mine did. He kept a fresh cut that always showed his natural waves. The only facial hair he had was a mustache. He could have been a model if he wasn't attracted to the streets.

"My brother is a law abiding citizen of Chicago who does no wrong." I couldn't keep a straight face when I told that lie. Kee got up and sat at another table. "Why you move?"

"I don't want to be near you when God strike you down for lying. Shame on you."

"Get back over here. I'm taking you with me."

Kee laughed and walked back over to the table I was sitting at. "So what's the plan for Zell?"

"We can easily just set him up one day. I think that would be too easy. I want to make him think everything is all good with us, then make him pay for everything he did. I want to make him suffer. I just hope Baker is gon' be okay with this taking a few months to do."

"Uh, I don't think he will be okay with that. You told me how mad he was that you spent the night with him. You think he's going to be cool with you spending a few months' worth of time with Zell?" Kee was right I knew Baker would be mad, but I have my ways of convincing him to say yes to anything.

"I know Kee, but I want to play with his emotions like he played with mine and yours. Smiling in our face like he didn't cause us an extreme amount of pain. He took my baby and your man."

"Can I ask you something?" I already knew what Kee was about to ask me. I nodded. "Did you ever tell Starks that could have been his baby?" I knew it.

"No, I didn't. You know Kee, even though Zell did hurt me in many different ways, I always felt bad about my involvement with Starks."

"I don't know why. Zell did you dirty and Starks was fine as hell, mmm mmm mmm," Kee said as she licked her lips. "All that fineness sitting in a jail cell." Starks looked like a taller, lighter version of the rapper T.I. "I secretly wanted you and him to be together."

"We had an agreement. He gave me dick when I wanted it and he always wanted to give it to me."

"He would have treated you right."

She was right and had we met under different circumstances it might have been something. I actually liked Starks, timing was just all bad. I took a trip down memory lane at the mention of Starks' name…

When I walked out of the gas station, I noticed this tall sexy T.I. look-a-like. He even had pretty white teeth like him. He had on a pair of grey jeans, a white tee, a grey and red Bulls fitted hat, and a pair fire red Jordan 5's.

"Let me get forty on one," he said to the attendant. I looked over to the pump he paid for, sitting there was a shiny black Benz. I took one last look at that sexy specimen of a man before I walked towards Kee's house.

"Excuse me, can I get out and talk to you for a second?" I ignored him. "I just saw you at the gas station. I had to come shoot my shot."

Making eye contact with him I asked, "Are you following me?"

"You make it sound like I'm stalking," he smiled. "So, can I get out and talk to you?" There was something about him that I was extremely attracted to.

"Yes you can." When he got closer, he was much more attractive than I previously thought he was and he smelled good. The cologne he had on blended with his body chemistry perfectly. I prayed Kee had a pair of panties that she hadn't worn before, mine were soaked from the presence of this stranger.

"What's yo' name? I'm Starks." He extended his hand for me to shake it.

"Serenity," I said as he brought my hand up to his mouth to kiss it. I had to give it to him, his approach was on point. Not too many people knew my real name, so if he ever told anybody about me they wouldn't think it was me.

"So, what's up? Can I get yo' number?"

"Well, I have a man."

"I don't have nothing to do with all that, I want to get to know you. What you got with him is you and his business. If something happens with us, it's gon' be our business. You feel me?"

I want to feel you is what I wanted to say, instead, I opted for, "Hand me your phone." I locked my number in and said, "Always text, never call." His pearly whites were all I saw.

"Alright." He kissed my hand one last time before he got back in his car and pulled off.

When I got to Kee's house, I filled her in on the smooth man I'd just met. She was happy I was contemplating dealing with somebody other than Zell. We talked for hours until I got a text from a number I didn't recognize.

Thinking about you.

I automatically knew it was Starks because that's the only unknown number that would pop up in my phone.

I responded with: Oh, really? I was just talking about you.

Seconds later he responded with: I want to see you.

I replied: I want to see you too. Meet me at the gas station we saw each other at earlier.

Be there in ten.

I had Kee drop me off at the gas station, Starks was already there waiting. When he spotted me, he pulled up on me. I got in his Benz and smiled at him.

"What's up, Serenity? You been on my mind heavy since

earlier."

Playing it cool, I said, "Is that right?"

"That's right. What you got planned for the night? I want to kick it wit' you." Noticing my hesitation he said, "I'm not gon' hurt you. I ain't that type of man."

"No, it's not that. It's just that I live with my man and I don't want to deal with him looking for me because I'm most definitely giving you my undivided attention tonight." I didn't mean to let that come out of my mouth. I just showed my thirst. Starks had me very parched. He smiled a hypnotizing smile that almost had me in love already. Forget Zell I was having fun tonight. He didn't come home the night before; he was just going to have to deal with me not being there.

"You know what let's just go, I'll deal with him when I see him."

"Whatever you want." When he pulled off the block, I called Kee to tell her to lock her door because I was gone for the night.

We talked the whole drive to his apartment. He lived in the Presidential Towers on Madison Street. His apartment had a color scheme of black and white, with hints of red here and there.

A sixty inch TV was mounted on his living room wall. His black leather couch sat back far enough so that you wouldn't go blind looking at his big TV.

He had two bedrooms and two bathrooms. One bedroom had a full sized bed, a dresser and a forty-two inch TV mounted on the wall, it had the feel of a guest room. Starks' bedroom had a king sized bed, a fifty inch TV on a smoke colored glass TV stand. His bedroom set was all black and white marble. His sheets were red and his comforter was black.

"This is nice."

"Thanks. I did this myself."

"Really? You could be an interior decorator."

"That money too slow for me. Bills ain't gon' wait."

"All you have to do is stack the fast money while you're in school, then when your name start ringing bells in the streets of interior design, you will be good."

"The streets of interior design, huh," he laughed. "You make that sound so easy."

"It will be easy for you, look around, you already got the

talent. I'm just trying to help you utilize it."

"Maybe one day. If I do, I know who I have to thank for it."
He looked at me with lust in his eyes. I would be lying to myself if
I said I didn't want to jump on his dick right now. "Oh, shit the
game on. You watch sports?"

"Only basketball. I love me some OKC." He frowned at that
statement like most people do.

"You gotta go. Nobody is allowed in my spot that's not a fan
of the home team."

Pretending I was leaving, I got off the couch and bolted to
the door. He grabbed my arm before I twisted the knob. "I
thought I had to go?" I asked as I looked in his eyes.

"I changed my mind I'mma make an exception for you."

"We watched the game together and talked shit to each other
the whole time. It was nice to kick it with somebody I could
actually talk to. I was so used to arguing with Zell all the time or
not talking to him at all, that I almost forgot how to have a
conversation.

Whenever I could get away, I spent time with Starks. I

enjoyed being around him. We had the best sex, it was like our bodies were made to please each other. Everything was perfect with our special friendship. It was a matter of time before something shook it up.

It was rare that Zell and I went out. On this one particular day, I wished he hadn't taken me anywhere. We went to the strip club for one of his friend's birthday. People from all over the city were out to celebrate the birth of Boog.

We went to a section of the club that was specifically for Boog and his guests. I looked around to see if I knew anybody there. I saw that smile that only Starks could smile. His smile faded when he saw Zell put his arm around my waist. His eyes asked me to confirm that Zell was my man. When I bowed my head that was all the confirmation he needed.

Zell mingled with people, while I conversed with a few females I knew. I could feel a pair of eyes on me from across the room. I was uneasy about being in the same room as two men that I was having sex with.

A text came to my phone: Meet me in the women's bathroom. NOW!

I walked to the bathroom not knowing if both of them were in there ready to whoop my ass or what. I pushed the door open to see someone leaning on the sink. I was less tense when I saw it was Starks.

"This bad. I didn't know you was Zell's girl."

"I didn't know you knew him. If I did, believe me I wouldn't have messed with you. I would never mess with one of his friends."

Starks looked me up and down, while licking his lips. "We grew up together. We not as close as we used to be back then. Damn. What we gon' do?"

"I don't want to end things between us. I love the way we get along and I'm not ready to give that up just yet." I didn't know what to do. I wanted to do what was right and end it, but I liked Starks. We got along so good, it was almost unreal. I contemplated ending things right then and there. I also thought about how comfortable I was with Starks as opposed to Zell. Starks pressed his lips up against mine gently as he palmed my ass with his hands.

"This crazy. It's a small world."

"Look, we can end it if that's what you want. Once I'm gone there is no coming back."

I was about to leave the bathroom when he grabbed me into one of the stalls. He lifted my dress up and exposed my neatly shaven pussy. He didn't have to do anything to get my juices flowing. For him, I dripped on sight. He eased his long, thick dick inside of me. I lightly moaned as he sent me to heaven with his strokes.

"Damn," he said a little too loud.

"Shhhh." I put my finger up to his lips.

"Damn, Serenity."

"You still want to end it?"

"Naw, if I did I would have let you walk out. We just gotta be real careful now."

"We're already careful. Just keep giving me some when I want it."

"You a trip. You know I'mma always give it to you."

With that being said, I got a paper towel to clean myself up.

When I found Zell, he was drunk and ready to go. I shot Starks a smile as I exited the club with an intoxicated Zell. I practically had to carry Zell up to our apartment. When we got there, I took a shower while he was passed out on the floor.

During the middle of the night, I felt a hand slap my ass. Jumping at the thought of it being a stranger, I felt relieved when it was Zell standing over me. His dick was hard and he had a lustful look in his eyes. We hadn't had sex for a couple months, he couldn't possibly pick tonight to want some.

"Come on Zell I'm tired tonight."

Zell didn't utter a word to me as he stuffed his dick inside of me and pounded me like it was the last time. I prayed that I wouldn't get pregnant. Fuckin' two men in the same night was not normal activity for me.

God must have been busy because my prayer went unanswered. Three months later, I found out I was pregnant. When the Doctor called me, my phone would only work if I had people on speaker. Zell was in the shower when I got the phone call. It was beyond me how he heard the conversation.

"You gon' keep that baby?" Zell asked as he stepped in the

bedroom in nothing except for a towel.

"What?" Zell wanted kids by me and I refused to give him any. Our relationship wasn't the best. Having a baby by him would only be a way for him to try to keep me around.

"Are you gon' keep that baby? I heard that whole conversation. You should have just went to her office if you didn't want me to know." He knew I didn't want a baby by him. That's one thing I never hid from him.

My thoughts drifted to Starks. What was I going to tell him? Truthfully, I didn't care who it belonged to. As much as I thought about it, I couldn't kill it. That would be a heartless thing to do.

When Zell got wind of me meeting Cash, I was relieved he asked Starks to follow me. I knew Starks' motive for following me. He wanted to make sure I wasn't actually messing around with Cash. As long as Zell had Starks watching me, he would never think to have someone watch Starks. One night after meeting up with Cash I told Starks I needed to talk to him.

"I'm pregnant."

Starks sat in silence for what seemed like forever before he spoke, "I told you that was gon' happen. How far are you?"

"It's not yours," I told half of a lie. I didn't know whose baby it was, so I lied to him. Telling him that I was further along than what I really was. The disappointment on his face came as a shock to me.

"So you about to have a baby on me, huh?"

"I don't want his baby. I can't get an abortion, this baby is just as much a part of me as it is his. At one point, I loved him so much, couldn't nobody tell me anything about him. All the cheating and lying is beginning to take a toll on me."

"Why stay with him if it's like that?"

"Convenience."

"You don't have to be with him. Come stay wit' me whenever you ready."

"We will talk more about me staying with you."

For the next couple of weeks, Starks asked me repeatedly was I pregnant with his baby, I always told him no. I couldn't tell him after I had sex with him in the bathroom of a club I slept with Zell hours later. He asked me what I wanted him to tell Zell about Cash. I told him to tell him what he saw. Neither of us *knew at the time what Zell had in store for me.*

We talked a little more about me coming to stay with him. I was tempted to do just that. Unfortunately, Starks caught a case before I lost the baby.

"You ready, Cola?" Kee asked, snapping me out of my trance.

"Yeah, let's go." Picking up all our bags, we left the mall.

When we got back home, I called Jay to see where he and Londyn were. He told me they had to go out to Schaumburg to shop, since he was supposed to be dead he didn't want to risk being seen with Londyn. Most likely, Jay and Londyn were going to stay the night at Marlene's house since she lived out there. I talked to Londyn for a second before she dropped the phone to pick up a toy. After I hung up with them, I texted Zell to let him know I wasn't going to be able to see him tonight. He never responded and I proceeded to get ready for my night with Baker.

Cola

It had been a couple days since I heard from Zell. I was enjoying the time I was getting to spend with Londyn and Baker anyway. We decided we would take Londyn to Baker's Aunt Carla's house while we took care of this situation with Zell. Miss Carla was excited to have Londyn come stay with her for a while. She had recently retired from the Police Department, she was all for keeping Londyn. As soon as we dropped Londyn off, she had Miss Carla wrapped around her finger like everybody else. She convinced Miss Carla to take her to get some ice cream ten minutes after she got there. Baker and I watched as Miss Carla became Londyn's prey.

"I need to talk to you," I said once we made it home.

Baker put his phone down. "What up baby?"

"This thing with Zell might take a couple months."

"Nah, not gon' happen, Cola."

"I want him to suffer. He took my baby, he took Duke from Kee, and set you up." I kissed his bald head to soften him up a little. "I want him to think everything is good then you and Jay can do whatever after that." I lifted his shirt and began to kiss his chest. "Two months baby." He moaned as I found my way to mini Baker. When I was done with Baker, he pulled me up face to face with him.

"I don't want you around that nigga. The thought of him touching you gets me mad."

"Baker, you know I won't let him touch me. I'mma make him think he gotta earn me back, then on the night he think he about to get some is the night he'll go to hell, literally."

"You got this all figured out, huh?" He kissed me on my forehead like he does every night when we lay down.

"I just came up with it as I was talking." We both laughed until Baker's phone lit up, it was his aunt Carla. I listened to make sure it was nothing with Londyn.

"They releasing him early...I thought he had a few more months to do...House Arrest?...You say Monday at 11?...Nah, I'll go get him, I know my lil lady driving you crazy.....That's Cola's fault always giving her what she want...A'ight I'll see y'all Monday after I pick him up."

"Don't be lying on me to, Miss Carla." Playfully, I slapped his arm. "Who you gotta pick up?"

"That punk ass slap hurt a lil bit. I gotta pick my cousin up for her. I know she wondering how both the men she raised ended up in the street life she tried to keep us away from." Baker always told me about his cousin. I felt like I knew him already.

"It just happens like that sometimes. I'm glad your cousin is coming home. I know from stories you told me that you and him were close."

"Yeah, we were. I haven't talked to him for four years. He didn't wanna socialize wit' nobody in the streets while he locked up. I have his pops send him some bread every week for me."

"That was smart of him. Don't think you about to be out all times of the night when he come home either."

"Here you go," Baker laughed. "I ain't on that. Ain't nothing gon' keep me away from yo' crazy ass. I'm low key scared of you. You cut muthafuckas in public. Ain't no telling what you will do to me in private."

"I swear I wish you would stop saying that." Baker always joked about what happened at his picnic. I wasn't proud of it, but Baker made me laugh about it.

We stayed up and talked for a few hours before we went to bed. Sometimes I wondered if getting even with Zell was even worth it. When I wanted to say forget it, I thought about my baby. Regardless if it was Zell's or Starks', it was mine.

Everybody was willing to let things go after I had Londyn, until Zell went after Jay. If Zell would have let things be, none of us would be plotting against him right now. He took my baby and tried to take my brother from me. I couldn't let that go.

Jay

"I'm tired of sitting in this fuckin' house." Kee gave me a

side eye. "Kee, I ain't no house nigga, I'm supposed to be in the streets. This play dead shit is for the birds. I feel like I used to feel when mama used to put me on punishment." We fell out laughing at the thought of me peeking out the blinds when I couldn't go outside.

"Cola said she will be done in two months, tops. Eight weeks is not a long time."

"Two months? Fuck she need two months for? That's a long time to be around that snake ass nigga."

"To play him like he played everyone else."

"Man she better not be on no bullshit. I'mma beat her ass if I find out she secretly fuckin' wit' this nigga. Sister or not, I will kill her."

"She wouldn't do that, she got too much to lose. Baker already told her he would leave and take Londyn. I would be done with her and you talking about killing her."

"Baker told her that shit for real?"

"Yeah, he told her that the other day."

I knew Cola and Baker had a strong relationship. For him to

tell her that meant he wasn't feeling this at all. I hope she knew what she was doing. I couldn't wait to put Zell six feet under. My thoughts took me back to the night he caught me slippin'…

"I'm leaving, Jay. Call me in the morning."

"Aight." I watched Tasha's ass sway from left to right as she walked out the door. That girl was blessed wit' a body straight from Heaven. A God had to create a body like that. I wish she didn't have a big mouth. If she didn't, I would keep her around. After she left, I took a shower, ate, and then fell asleep.

In the middle of the night, I could have sworn I heard my door open and close. Too tired to check it out, I covered my head with my comforter and went back to sleep. About ten minutes later, I felt a presence in my room. Call it a real niggas intuition, but I was right. Within seconds, I felt somethin' sharp penetrate my side.

At first, I didn't feel any pain; all of a sudden I felt hot and dizzy, then came the pain. I kept still while I tried to think of what to do next. If I reached for my pistol whoever this was would know I wasn't dead. I was about to say fuck it then I heard footsteps walking away from me. I didn't know what the fuck was going on. I knew a nigga ain't just come stab me in my side and leave. I heard more footsteps in my living room. I wasn't going out like a sucker. I grabbed my pistol from under my bed and waited on whoever was in my crib.

"Finish him off, call me when it's done." I didn't recognize that voice. After the door shut, I heard two niggas talking.

"I ain't never killed nobody, Feek." Feek? I questioned myself. It dawned on me that it was Feek, the youngin' Zell sent my way.

"Me neither, Spook and we not gon' kill nobody today."

"I thought you was mad about him threatening yo' granny and sister."

"I am mad. I'm mad at myself for getting' mixed up with Zell. He the reason granny 'nim had to move. He used me because he knew I needed money." I listened as Feek talked to his friend.

"What we gon' do, Feek?"

"I don't know. If Jay come out here he probably gon' kill us. I need to think of something fast."

"Ain't nobody gon' kill y'all unless y'all try some fuck shit," I said as I walked up to them holding my bloody side. They both

jumped at the sound of my voice. "Zell sent y'all?"

Feek spoke up, "He said if we kill you he would pay us." My side began to throb and I started to feel dizzy. I called Marlene to come check me out while Feek talked.

"Did he tell you why?" I asked as I looked over at Feek's friend. He was quiet and looked at whoever was talking. I could tell he followed Feek's lead.

"He said that you shot him in his sleep a few years back. He wanted us to come in after he stabbed you, stab you in both eyes, and leave the knives there, and he wanted us to shoot you in the chest."

"Word?" I rubbed my chin.

"Yeah."

"What he say he gon' pay y'all for this?"

"Twenty stacks." I chuckled at that. "Jay, I need that money bad. I got a girl and a son to take care of."

"Do you think twenty stacks is a big enough pay off to take a man's life?"

"No," Feek said while his sidekick shook his head from side to side.

"If you gon' kill a nigga get a hundred stacks or better." Marlene got there to check on me. I didn't have any major damage, she patched me up, gave me some pain pills and told me to go to the hospital as soon as I was done here. "Because you was honest I ain't gon' kill y'all. Wait right here." I kept a safe in my bedroom for emergencies. It held three hundred thousand dollars at all times. I put a hundred stacks in a book bag.

"What we gon' tell Zell?" Feek asked as I walked back in the living room.

"Call him and tell him it's done. I'mma disappear for a while. Take this money." I tossed Feek's friend the book bag. Their eyes widened when they saw the amount of money in that bag. "When he pay y'all what he owe y'all, either kill him or leave Chicago because I will be back and if he finds out y'all didn't kill me he gon' come for y'all."

"Call him, Spook, tell him we did it." While Spook made the call, Feek told me he had never seen this much money before. I told him he played for the wrong team when he got wit' Zell. He should have come to me in the first place and money like that would be like pennies to him.

"When he pay, text this number, and let me know if he dead or if y'all leaving." I passed Feek a piece of paper wit' my business number on it. I gave them more than enough money to start their own operation in another state. All they had to do was find a connect wherever they decided to go.

"We can go now?" Spook finally broke his silence.

When they left, I called Tasha to see if she had anything to do wit' this shit. I only spent the night in the city because of her. If I would have went home, I wouldn't have gotten stabbed. After threatening Tasha's kids, she still maintained her innocence.

Cola called right after I hung up with Tasha, she cursed me out and told me she was on her way to get me. I told Cola everything Feek told me. That's when we decided we needed to come back. Cola said she wasn't about to let him get another chance to kill me. Kee kept her old house when we moved to DeKalb, so we already had somewhere to stay. The same day we came to the city, Cola went to every block Tara told Baker Zell sold dope on until she found him. Now we was waiting on her to give us the word.

"Here," Kee interrupted my thoughts to pass me the blunt she had just rolled.

"Two damn months, I might as well be locked up." I inhaled the smoke from the blunt, then passed it back to Kee.

"That's how you messed up the last time, being in a rush. You would think with her being a nurse she would have known exactly where to shoot him. I would hate for her to be my nurse."

"It's about aim, too. I took Marlene to the gun range plenty of times to get her prepared to shoot that nigga. Her aim was decent at the range, we both thought she was ready. Shooting a piece of paper is different from shooting a body."

"Whatever, Jay."

"Man, she was nervous. If I didn't know no better I would swear you was being a hater."

"A hater is the last thing I'll be. You should have did it yourself or got somebody that wouldn't be nervous."

"Girl get naked and be quiet."

"I can't believe these niggas just up and left my block to run itself. It's been a week and nobody has seen or heard from these muthafuckas," I said to Anaya. I knew I was supposed to leave her, but after that fight we had, Anaya said Peachy was coming back for a week.

For the whole week we were fuckin' like the world was gon' end. Every time I tried to check my phone, Peachy or Anaya would end up distractin' me. I got some other niggas runnin' things, but I don't trust them.

"Why are you talking to me? My cute ass is about to go find another man since you leaving." I don't know why I tried to talk to her. We barely said two words to each other this week. All we did was fuck, eat, and sleep.

"Good luck wit' that." I grabbed my bags and left.

As soon as I got in the car, I texted Cola that I wanted to see her. I rode in silence to my crib on Lake Shore Drive. Wore out from Peachy and Anaya, I fell asleep on the couch as soon as I got there. An hour later, I jumped up when my phone rang; it was Cola. "I'm up north...I left her...She ain't care she already talkin' about findin' another nigga to take care of her...So what's up you comin' through?...A'ight call me when you downstairs."

"Where you been all week?" Cola asked when she saw me. She was lookin' good. She had on some skin tight white skinny jeans with rips from the thighs to the knees, showin' a tease of the tattoo she had on her thigh. Her black tank top fit her perfect set of D's perfectly. She had on some black and silver sandals that had her toes lookin' edible. Her red hair complemented her brown skin well. I missed her a lot, this time it was gon' be right.

"Shit just takin' care of things. Some niggas just left my block to run itself the other day. I had to be around to oversee these new niggas."

"Oh, okay boss man." I felt bad about where I had really been all week. I knew it was gon' be awhile before Cola let me hit, so I got my rocks off wit' Naya and Peachy all week. I did watch them new niggas for a day, though. "You got something to eat in here?"

"Hell naw, we can go grab somethin' or I can order somethin'." She asked me to order some pizza along wit' a Pepsi. "You still love that pop I see."

"You know I can't give up the pop." I laughed at the thought of the way she used to fiend for that shit like crack.

We ate and talked for a few hours before she was ready to go. It felt like old times and when I say old times, I mean the times we had when we first met. Our first year together was perfect, she had a nigga wantin' to marry her ass. Tara used to clown me and I started bein' reckless wit' my shit. I regretted some of the shit I did to her. It was one thing I did that I know if she knew I did she wouldn't be sittin' here today. I know for a fact she would beat Kee's ass.

"I don't want you to leave. You can't stay the night with me?"

"I can't, I promised Kee I would go to this club with her. I have to go get ready."

"What club y'all goin' to?"

"The Shrine for some guy she knows party." I stared at Cola imaginin' how good she was gon' look in whatever she had on. I had to go to go that club tonight.

"You mind if I come through?" She thought about it and told me it was cool for me to stop through.

"That pop ran right through me." Cola stood to go to the washroom. I jumped up when I remembered the bottle of pills I had on the sink.

"Wait." I ran to the bathroom before she took a step. I stuffed the pill bottle in my pocket then ran some water in the sink.

"Zell, I really have to use the bathroom."

"I'm cleanin' up I had dirty clothes all over the floor."

"Right now I could care less about some dirty clothes on the floor. All I want to do is empty my bladder."

I opened the door. "It's all yours."

"Thanks."

Cola stayed wit' me for another hour. When she was ready to go, I walked her downstairs to her car. She was pushin' a white Range Rover wit' tints. As she pulled off, I caught a glimpse of the license plate. I gotta ask her what that mean the next time I talk to her.

Cola

"Zell said he coming tonight," I said as I walked in the house. Jay, Baker, and Kee were sitting in the living room watching SpongeBob. I knew they were high out of their minds. That was the only time they watched cartoons or when Londyn was around.

"Move sis Sandy Cheeks got cheeks. You blocking my view." I could have punched Jay in the nose.

"Jesus, Mary, and, Joseph you need help." I looked at Baker who was sitting in a chair on mute. I knew what was bothering him. "Baker, you wanted it done soon. I got him coming to the club tonight."

"Mmmhmmm." As I walked towards him he suddenly got up and went in the bedroom. I didn't know what his problem was. He needed to take it out on whoever did it to him because it wasn't me.

"What is wrong with you?" I asked as he sat on the bed.

"Ain't shit wrong wit' me? What's wrong wit' you taking my car to see that nigga. Sometimes you don't think, Serenity."

"You mad about a car? If my car wasn't in the shop, I would have driven my own. You just being petty because you don't want me around him. I told you I won't slip."

"You not gon' slip?"

"No, I'm not. Baker, you don't have any faith in me." I was

pissed Baker was acting like this over me taking his car. He shouldn't have gave me the extra key if he didn't want me to use his car.

"I have faith in you, but you ain't thinking rationally."

Yelling I said, "All I did was take your damn car!!!"

"First, watch who you talking to in that loud ass voice. Second, did you think about the plates on the car? Third, did you notice what's engraved on the headrests? Fourth, did you make sure he didn't see none of that shit?" I thought about everything Baker just said. I had indeed messed up. His plates read, "BAKE1" and the headrests each had a name. "Baker" was engraved on the driver side, "Cola" was on the passenger side, "Londyn" was on the back driver side, and the letter "J" was on the back passenger side in representation of the baby I lost. I didn't think about any of that when I took his car.

"Baker I slipped." No excuses were made. I did it and I admitted it.

"No shit Sherlock and you got his bitch ass coming to my party. How the fuck I'mma enjoy my b-day wit' that savage ass nigga in my party running around behind my girl?"

"I'm sorry, Baker." I thought I would be helping speed up the process. That was what they wanted and that was what I was giving them, now he mad. I can't win for losing.

Before he left our room he said, "You need to un-invite that nigga. I'm not gon' spend my night watching him act like what's mine is his."

Baker was furious with me. I understood why. If Zell put two and two together he would know Baker was somewhere around me. I called Zell to tell him I wasn't coming out tonight after all. His phone was going straight to the voicemail. Having no other choice, I left a voicemail saying that I was staying home.

Baker was having a party tonight to celebrate twenty seven years of living. We made up before we left the house. Baker looked good in his white Robin's jeans and white button up shirt with a white and gold Gucci belt. He completed his look with a pair of white and gold Gucci sneakers and a white and gold Gucci beanie. I wore a short strapless form fitting white Gucci dress with a pair of white and gold open toed Gucci pumps.

"Baby, you got it packed out here," I said to Baker when we pulled up to a long line of cars blocking traffic on Wabash Street.

"Probably don't know half of these niggas." He pulled his black Maserati GranTurismo up to the front door of the club. We got out while the valet he hired for the night jumped in to park the car.

As soon as we stepped in the club, Young Jeezy's song *Hustlaz Ambition* started playing. That was Baker's favorite song ever since it came out years ago. He played it every morning when he left the house to hit the streets.

Baker didn't want his own section in the club, he wanted every person there to feel equal. Everybody that entered 'The Shrine' got a free drink as soon as they walked in. Cîroc and Patron were our drinks of choice. Baker didn't follow trends and I loved that about him. He could have easily had bottles of expensive liquor around him, but he left that to the niggas that wanted to be seen. Baker was the type that only wanted to be heard.

He looked around the club to see if anybody looked suspicious. After he scanned the crowd he said, "Told you I don't know half these people. I only see a few familiar faces."

"That's because you mean."

"No, I ain't, I just like to keep my circle small." He placed his hand on the small of my back while we maneuvered through the crowd. "I know 'em, but I don't know 'em like that. That small crowd of niggas coming in the door as we speak are really the only ones I cared about coming besides you, Jay, and Kee. I wanted my cousin here. He got one day and a wake up left in the joint."

I looked at the group of men entering the club to see Jake, Bubba, Goo, Trell, Maine, and Big Curt. All of the men he hustled with day in and day out, except Trell and Maine. They were brothers and friends of Baker's from Philly. Trell and Maine were making major money in Philly. They missed Baker's party last year, so they made sure they made it to this one.

Big Curt hardly ever showed his face at clubs. He was Baker's connect and they became close friends over the years. Most connects only supplied work, not Big Curt. When it came to Baker, he would be right on the frontlines ready for whatever.

"Kee and Jay coming in. I gotta go talk to Kee real quick," I said to Baker.

"A'ight."

Jake and everybody else made their way to where we were. I spoke to everybody and gave Big Curt a hug. Walking over to Kee, I felt someone touch my thigh. I snatched away and went off on him for touching me. I looked back at Baker who was smiling at me. I winked and smiled back at him.

"Kee, you got that for me?" Earlier I asked Kee to pick up the gift I bought Baker for his birthday. I was nervous about giving it to him. I wasn't sure if he would like it or not.

"Yes ma'am, I have it in my purse. Jay was jealous." I knew he would be mad when he saw it. I'll have to do something special for my baby brother.

"Let me see it." I was so excited about his gift, you would think it was mine. "That's hot. You think he'll like it, Kee?" I asked wondering if I did too much.

"I will gladly take it to the pawn shop if he don't."

"You crazy. Let's go see his reaction." I strutted my way back over to Baker and everybody else. Jay had a fake mean mug on his face as I walked to Baker. I gave him the puppy dog eyes and he smiled at me and waved his hand. I grabbed Baker's arm to get his attention.

"I have your gift." He looked confused because I gave him a gift earlier. That was nothing, but a few pairs of his favorite jeans, and some cologne.

"What you talking about, didn't you give me my gift earlier?"

"That wasn't the real gift, here." I handed him the red velvet box with a black bow tied around it. He untied the bow and opened the box. His eyes almost popped out of their socket when he saw the white gold, six carat, round cut diamond pinky ring. He told me he has wanted one ever since he lost his father's ring.

This ring was a tribute to his father. I knew he wouldn't wear the ring often. I wanted him to have it for the memory of his father who got shot and killed when Baker was only ten years old. A year after his father was killed his mother died of a heart attack. Both Baker and Miss Carla said she really died of a broken heart because she never got over the death of her husband. Miss Carla stepped in and raised Baker after he lost his mother.

"You like it?"

"I love it, Co, thank you. Damn, you even had a couple of

blue diamonds put in it." Blue was his father's favorite color. It was only right that I had my jeweler customize the ring with blue diamonds scattered here and there. "Man baby I don't even know what to say."

"Don't say anything, Baker. Enjoy your night and know that I love you."

Jake walked over to Baker to get a closer look at the ring. "You need to marry her."

"I agree," Big Curt chimed in. "She's one of a kind, Baker."

"Tell him again!" I shouted. I grabbed Kee to go to the bar. "I'm happy he liked it. He has never been speechless before."

"Ummmmm, I think he about to be speechless again."

"Why you say that?" I asked not knowing what Kee was talking about.

"Zell just walked in."

"What?!?!?! I left him a message and told him I wasn't coming out. Why is he here, Kee?" Glancing in the direction Baker was in, I could tell by the angry look on his face that he saw Zell walk in.

"You know he crazy. He probably popped up just to see if you was here or not."

Just as I was about to walk away, I saw Zell walking towards Baker. Zell held his hand out for Baker to shake, Baker stared at it for a second, then shook it. I nervously looked around for Jay, if Zell saw him all hell would break loose. "Where did Jay go that fast?"

"Jay is always aware of his surroundings. He must have saw him and left."

"I need to make sure he safe." I pulled out my phone to call Jay. "Where you at?...Thank God you saw him, you really need to stay in the house...I don't care how bored you are...You know that the sooner we take care of this the better...Okay...Are you going to stay off the radar?...Text me when you make it home."

"I assume he saw him," Kee stated.

"Yeah, he did. Kee lets go before Zell spots me." As we left, I wondered what Zell and Baker were talking about. I sent Baker a text once we got in his Maserati: *I left before he saw me. I promise I left him a voicemail saying I wasn't coming tonight. I don't know why he came. I took the car. Can you get home?*

Baker responded five minutes later: *I know you cancelled on him he said "his bitch" cancelled at the last minute and he decided to come out because somebody told him it was my party....I'm good Big Curt gon' drop me off.*

I was relieved Baker knew I was being honest. This situation had him questioning my judgment. Zell called me his bitch like we had something going on. He was a disrespectful dickhead.

Sleep didn't come easy for me because Baker didn't come home. Baker had never come after the sun was out. Pissed wasn't the word for what I was. When I rolled over at 6 a.m. to a cold spot on the bed, I was up with some scissors and his socks cutting the big toe out of all of them.

I rolled them all back up and stuffed them back in the sock drawer. At 7 a.m., I was cutting holes in the underarms of all his shirts and in the back of his boxers. Just doing little petty stuff I knew would make him mad. At 8 a.m., I was ready to bleach every pair of Jordan's, Air Force Ones, Prada, Gucci, and any other type of shoe he owned sitting in the middle of the floor. Before I could destroy them, I heard a car door slam. I sat on the edge of the bed and waited.

"Where the fuck you been?"

"What you got my shoes sitting out here like this for?" Baker saw the bleach on the floor. "You about to wash? Throw these clothes in there." He changed into a pair of white and red basketball shorts and a white t-shirt.

"No, muthafucka'. Where in the fuck have you been? You been out all night doing what?"

"Calm down, Co." He began picking his shoes up to put them back in the closet. "I been wit'…" I slapped the shoes out of his hands before he finished his sentence.

"Out with some bitch? Is that where you and him been? It's 8 in the fuckin' morning and you walking in here all cool like shit all good. You got me fucked up, Baker."

"It's too early for this bullshit."

"It's too early? It's too early for you to be walking in this house like you single. Maybe I should call Zell, spend the whole day and night with him. I'm sure he would lo…." Before I could get my last words out, I felt the collar of my shirt get snug around my neck.

Baker grabbed me by my shirt and pulled me close to him. "Bitch, if you ever in yo' fuckin' life threaten me wit' that nigga or any other nigga I will kill yo' ass three times." Baker gripped my shirt tighter. "You think that shit you just said to me is cool? Go be wit' him if you want to, watch what happens to both of y'all. I was with Big Curt at the hospital. My Godson was born at 6:30 this morning. We stayed at the hospital then went out to breakfast." Finally, letting go of my shirt he said, "You starting to piss me the fuck off, straight up."

"Why didn't you call if that's where you was at? And why didn't you say that when you first got here." I sat on the bed not knowing what emotion to feel. Baker never grabbed me like that before or called me any disrespectful names. Not to my face anyway. We always had respect for each other. At that point, I knew I went too far with what I said. All he had to do was tell me Big Curt's girl, Kimmy, had the baby.

"If yo' phone wasn't going right to voicemail you would have known that. I called Jay's phone for you, he said you were sleep and he would tell you as soon as you got up. How can I tell you anything? When I walked in, you all down my throat? You know that nigga was at the party last night. Some shit could have went down and he could have killed me or I could have killed him and you in here thinking I'm laid up wit' another woman."

Baker shook his head and put his shoes up.

Baker was right. It never crossed my mind that him and Zell could have killed each other. Baker had never given me a reason to think he was cheating on me. In my mind, my thoughts were justified for the simple fact that he'd never stayed out all night. Any normal woman would have thought the same thing I did.

I heard a knock at the door. It was Jay. "Aye, sis you up?" Jay asked on the other side of the closed door.

"Yeah, Jay."

Jay walked in saying, "Baker at the hospital wit' Big Curt…." He noticed Baker and stopped talking to me. "Damn, when you come in, Baker?" He looked at both of our faces. "What's up wit' y'all?"

"You about to leave?" Baker asked Jay.

"Nah, I'm dead, I can't make no moves. Why? What's up?" Jay frowned.

"I need to use yo' room to get some sleep. I can't be around yo' sister right now. She on some other shit bruh."

"Go ahead," Jay said as he looked at me confused.

I grabbed Baker's arm before he reached the door. He snatched away from me and said, "Let me fuckin' go man! Go grab Zell's arm since you threatening to go lay up under him." Baker walked out of the room pissed off.

"Damn sis, what happened? I've never seen him that mad at you." I explained everything to Jay. I left out the part about Baker grabbing me, Jay would kill him or die trying. He got on me about jumping to conclusions and shooting the bullets out my pistol of a mouth. Sometimes it was good, other times it was not. Jay let me cry on his shoulder until my tears stopped flowing. "You cool now?" he asked as I stood to look in the mirror.

"No. I can't be mad at nobody but myself. He was right I didn't give him a chance to tell me where he was. I automatically went off on him."

"Co, you gotta stop living in the past. Baker a good guy. You was wrong for what you said to him and I'm sort of mad at you for that."

"What if he leaves me, Jay?" I asked, beginning to cry again at the thought of losing Baker.

"That nigga not going nowhere. Talk to him later, after he

wakes up and cool down. Stop crying, shit making me feel all weird inside." I let out a laugh as he tried to shake off the emotions he was feeling. "Man I didn't think I was ever gon' get you to laugh after all the snot and boogers you just cried on my shoulder."

"Shut up," I smiled. "Thanks Jay."

"Don't thank me, that's my job as a brother. I love you sis, I never wanna see you upset or hurt."

"I love you, too, Jay." Although I know Jay loves me, he doesn't tell me often. I reached over to give him a tight hug.

"Get off me, I'm done being an emotional thug," he laughed. "You and him will be good after he cools off."

"I hope."

"Y'all will. Aye, let's watch some movies."

"Okay, but I want to call Londyn first, I miss my baby."

I called Miss Carla and she answered on the first ring telling me I can't have Londyn back yet and she would take her to Mexico to prevent us from taking her. She was really enjoying Londyn. I talked to Londyn for about ten minutes. I told her I loved her and would be there to see her first thing in the morning. Miss Carla got back on the phone and told me to have Baker call her as soon as he got up. I texted Baker the message his aunt told me to relay.

Watching movies with Jay reminded me of back in the day when we were kids. Jay, Kee, my mother, and I would watch movies, play games, and eat junk food all day. Even when we all grew up and moved out, every Sunday we went to my mother's house to eat a home cooked meal and hear the adventures my mother had with the men she encountered in her life before she met my father.

Jay didn't want to hear any of that. When Baker came around, my mother called him her other son. She refused to move to DeKalb with us until Londyn came along. My mother loved her so much, she came to pick her up at some point every day until the day she died. Words couldn't describe how much I missed my mother.

"You got snacks, Jay?" I asked walking back in the room.

"Hell yeah. If I can't leave the house I need to have everything I need. The only thing that's missing is some in house pussy."

"How many times do I have to tell you I'm your sister, not your brother?" I smacked him on the head.

"Sometimes I wonder." We both laughed. Jay tossed me the black plastic bag full of every junk food ever made. He brought in five more bags full of chips, candy, pop, and juice.

"You about to make me get fat with all this junk."

"Bitches get fat everyday B." I burst out with the loudest laugh, he was acting like one of the characters from the movie we were about to watch. We sat on the floor surrounded by junk food.

"Cut me in or cut it out!" Kee shouted from the doorway. "Where's Baker?" she asked.

Kee sat on the floor Indian style sifting through the sea of junk. I told her what happened this morning. She agreed with what Jay said about Baker needing to calm down.

We proceeded to watch the movie. My mind would drift to Baker until Jay cracked a joke to make me cheer up. Even though I had Baker on my mind I had a ball with Jay and Kee.

Day turned into night before Jay and Kee exited my room.

Soon after they left, I crawled into bed. I couldn't help but think about Baker. He'd never been that mad at me. I was mad at him for what he did, but I hope he forgave me for what I said. Eventually, I drifted off into a deep sleep.

Baker

This bed feels like feathers; I thought to myself as I stood up to stretch. I checked my phone and noticed I had a few missed calls and a couple texts. I called my Aunt Carla first. She wanted to remind me not to be late picking her son up in the morning. I talked to Londyn for a few minutes. She told me she made me a picture to keep in my car.

I called Big Curt back next, he told me he found out who Zell's girl Anaya was. I told him to have Jake get her number and entertain her for a couple weeks just in case we needed her. Stepping out of Jay's room into the darkness of the house, I noticed bodies on the couch. I got a lil closer and saw Jay and Kee hugged up on the couch. I cut the light on, they both jumped up trying to play it off.

"Damn Baker I thought you was Cola," Jay said while Kee sat still looking nervous.

"What up doe? What y'all got goin' on?"

"Don't tell my sister."

"Please don't tell her, Baker. I don't know how she will take it," Kee spoke with uneasiness in her voice.

"How long this been going on?" They both looked at each other.

"We've been off and on since before I started living with them," Kee said.

"Get the fuck outta here. Was this going on when you and Duke was together?"

"No Baker, I loved Duke with all my heart. Jay and I were on bad terms when I met Duke. I caught Jay out East with some girl and I left him alone after that. He tried to come back, but I was already feeling Duke and didn't want anything to do with Jay. Keep this a secret for now, I want to be the one to tell Cola. Do you think it's weird that we together after I was basically raised as his sister?"

"No because y'all started before you moved in wit' them. It's not like y'all waited until y'all was grown."

"I hope Cola sees it that way also," Kee said.

Jay was staring off in space, I wanted to know what was on his mind. "You good bruh?"

"Man you and my sister need to fix what y'all going through. The way y'all relationship is, made me want to stop fuckin' wit' Marlene and all the other broads. I want to take shit wit' Kee seriously. You gon' holla at her, Baker?"

"I don't know bruh. I can't even look at her after what she said. Cola was dead ass wrong for that."

Kee came to the defense of her best friend. "You know she said it out of anger. She didn't mean it, Baker."

"Yeah aight. I'm going to spend the night wit' Londyn tonight. I still don't wanna see y'all sister."

"Aw shit, let the jokes begin," Jay said.

"That's the truth." Retrieving the keys to my Range Rover, I left the house.

I was still hot about that dumb shit Cola said to me. I was madder at myself for reacting the way I did. Cola ain't never pissed me off to the point that I had to grab her or call her anything, but her name. I felt fucked up about that shit.

I made it to my aunt's house at about 11:30 p.m. My nostrils led the way to her house. Aunt Carla stayed having the block smelling good from her cooking.

"Boy you scared me. What are you doing here nephew?" Aunt Carla was in the kitchen cooking fish and spaghetti.

"Me and Cola had a bad argument. Londyn sleep?"

"Yes she is. I wore her little butt out at the park earlier. She's ball of fun, you two are really blessed."

"If Cola keeps tryin' me she gon' tear our family apart."

"Boy, what happened that got you talking like that after you gave me a ring to hold for her?" I told her everything, leaving nothing out. Even though she was a former officer of the law, she would never turn her back on her son or me. She didn't agree wit' the stuff we did, so she turned a blind eye and deaf ear to it. "Lord when are you and your cousin going to learn that the streets are no good for you? When you were out in DeKalb, you and Cola had a fairytale life. Now that you've come back, the problems have started. Hurry up and take care of this situation, so you can go back to having a peace of mind."

"What situation needs to be taken care of?" my uncle asked walking into the house.

"What up doe, Unc?"

"What it is, Nephew? If you came to pick up my niece you can forget it. She can't leave yet."

"Nah, Unc, needed to get away."

B Starks was the most dangerous hitman in the streets of Chicago back in the 70's and 80's. My aunt had a thing for dangerous men. She had to keep her marriage a secret while she was on the force. Now that she was retired, they were able to go out whenever and wherever they wanted.

"You got a problem, Nephew?"

"Oh, lord," Aunt Carla sighed.

"Say Slim, be easy, we just talking." B Starks was still smooth even in his 60's.

"A woman, Unc."

B had his eyes glued to my aunt while he spoke. "Young blood a woman is never a problem. A woman is a man's rib," he said, just before my aunt walked out of the kitchen smiling. B looked down the hallway to make sure my aunt was in her room. "I thought she would never leave. I was just jivin' young blood. What's the word?" I laughed and told him everything that was going on wit' me and Co. B told me most likely dealing wit' Zell got old emotions running wild in her mind. "Do me a solid, Nephew."

"What you need, B?"

"Keep ya' cousin out of trouble, roll ya' ole Unc up a joint, and call me a young tender to meet later on."

"Hell nah. Auntie Carla will make me disappear if I did that."

"Just jivin'," he grinned, "Slim is a hell of a woman. I was serious about the other two things."

"I got him. Starks won't go back if I can help it."

This nigga B is a fool; I thought to myself as I rolled his joint up. We sat and talked for an hour before I went to the room Londyn was in. I kissed her on the forehead then fell asleep on the floor right next to the twin sized bed she was sleeping in.

I woke up to Londyn opening and closing my eyelids wit' her little fingers. Looking down at me, she flashed the prettiest smile I have ever seen. "Hey my favorite girl!" I said getting off the floor and on her bed.

"Hi, daddy. Mommy hewe?"

"No, she not. I thought you would be happy to see me and you asking for yo' mama." Pretending I was sad, I covered my face wit' my hands. She placed her little hands on top of mine to remove them from my face.

"I love you daddy." Even at a young age she cared how other people felt.

"I love you, too, baby girl. You wanna ride wit' me today to go pick up your cousin?"

"Yesssssssssssss!!"

"Now we gon' be in the car for a long time, are you sure you wanna go?"

"Yes daddy. Can we go get a toy?"

"Anything for you. I gotta get Aunt Carla to do your hair and get you dressed, but first you gotta eat. Go wake her up to cook for us." Londyn ran to Aunt Carla's room.

I could hear B say, "Princess, you jivin'." He still talked like he did when we were growing up. I sat on the couch until my aunt came to the kitchen to make breakfast. I asked her to get Londyn ready because I was taking her with me.

An hour later, I strapped Londyn in her booster seat and hit the road. We had a two hour drive ahead of us to Dixon Correctional Center. We stopped at the store for her toys, chips, and juice. At 11:15 a.m., I pulled up to the prison. Londyn was holding her new doll in the back. "I wanna eat daddy. I don't want chips."

"Aight baby girl we can get some food as soon as we leave here." I shook my head. Londyn had me buy all this junk now she was saying she didn't want it. I'm not mad at my baby girl, though.

"Okay, I'm sleepy." I looked back at her barely able to keep her eyes open, yet she still managed to say she was hungry.

"Go to sleep I promise when you wake up you will have some chicken nuggets."

"Okay daddy," she said, drifting off to sleep.

Another 20 minutes passed before he finally came out. He walked out still looking the same. Being gone for damn near four years should have put some weight on him.

"What's up cuzzo?" he said as he sat in the passenger's side of my Range.

"The infamous Kevin Starks. Son of that nigga B. Starks. What up doe cuz, wit' yo' T.I. looking ass."

"Cut it out, I don't look like him. Man I'm glad to be outta there. Who is the light skinned chick in the back?" he joked, looking back at Londyn.

"That's yo' cousin, Londyn."

"I ain't believe Pops when he told me you had a lil one. She is gorgeous. You sure she yours?" We both laughed.

"That's definitely mine. She got the eyes."

"I watched a lot of Maury over the years and umm, I'm messing with you. Who is her mama?"

"Man I don't wanna talk about her right now."

"You must not be with her."

"We still together. We just into it right now. She said some dirty shit to me yesterday and I grabbed her up. Called her a bitch and everything. I feel bad about that. You know I don't be on that wit' women. I had to go to yo' mama house last night."

"She had to have had you hot for you to grab her. I know you not about to throw y'all relationship away over some words. Whatever she said can't be that bad."

"Nah, I ain't gon' throw it away, she mean a lot to me. I

needed too cool down. I'mma go talk to her after I drop y'all off." I peeked at Londyn still sleeping through my rear view mirror.

"So, what's up in the streets?" I filled Starks in on everything that was going on and everything I found out about Zell. "He set you up and killed Duke? Niggas don't know what loyalty is out here. I'm itchin' to get him."

"Starks you fresh out the joint, I'm not gon' put you in a position to go right back. My girl got beef wit' him for making her lose her baby. I'm trying to do things her way. I ain't gon' lie, when that nigga came to my party I was gon' take care of him then. We lost the nigga in the crowd when everybody started leaving."

Starks protested, "Pops taught me everything I need to know. I wasn't locked up for none of my bodies. I had a drug charge. Zell pulled a lot of coward moves. He should have stopped breathing the day you touched down in the city." He was right about that. I think Cola suffered the most out of everybody, so it was only right that I honored her wishes.

"I feel you. We will talk more about it. Besides ain't you about to be on house arrest? How can you commit a murder when you can't even go on the porch? And I thought the Sherriff was supposed to bring you home today and set it up?"

"They coming to set it up in the a.m. I could get him tonight and be sleeping like a baby by the time they get there. I got my connections, Baker," he smirked.

"You a fool. You know yo' mama ain't letting you out today. Who you have to fuck to get that connection?"

"A Judge." Starks was as serious as a heart attack. "You right about my moms, she about to have me on a leash. I hope Pops stay in today, I can't deal wit' a lecture today from my ole girl." I felt his pain. Aunt Carla could go on for hours about the life we chose to live. I planned on being gone before she got started. B Starks was always our savior when she started with her talks.

"A judge? I wanna know about this. B was there when I left, if not Londyn will keep you company, she staying over there until we get through wit' Zell. If any harm comes her way I'mma leave this city red. I swear on my life."

"That was the baddest judge I had ever seen. We had her chambers held up for a minute. I already know how you would be about the lil one."

"You wild as hell nigga. I gotta stop at the restaurant for Londyn." I turned into the drive thru and ordered a chicken nugget happy meal, a burger for Starks, and a chicken sandwich for myself.

We reflected on old times, good and bad, on the ride back to Chicago. Londyn stayed sleep the whole time, I guess the ride was too long for her. As we pulled up, we inhaled the aroma of fried chicken, greens, corn, homemade mac and cheese, sweet potatoes, dressing, and buttermilk biscuits. I saw a custom painted, metallic blue Maserati GranTurismo just like mine pulling away from the curb.

"That paint job nice. I wonder what the interior look like." Starks was in awe of the color of the car. Cola's paint job made me wanna get mine painted a different color.

"The interior white."

"You seen the inside before?"

"That was my girl. The car was black until she saw a Lexus in that shade of blue. I surprised her wit' the paint job and white interior. When Zo got done wit' it, I was hatin' hard."

"Zo still doing his thing with the cars? He had my Benz right.

I miss that car."

"I got somethin' being worked on for you. It will be ready before you get off that box."

"Appreciate it, Baker."

"No, problem cuz."

Starks got Londyn out of the backseat of the car while I got her toys and food. We entered the house to a nice spread of food. My aunt embraced Starks for what seemed like an eternity before she let him go. Starks still had Londyn in his arms and the hug woke her up. She looked at Stark's face, then looked around the house to make sure she was in a familiar place. When she saw me, she reached for me.

"Oh, it's like that? You just gon' leave yo' big cousin like that?" Londyn put her head on my shoulder playing the shy role.

"That's Aunt Carla's son. His name Starks, say hi to your cousin."

"Hi," she said wit' her head still on my shoulder. Once Londyn warmed up to him she would talk his ear off. Starks loved kids, he would love Londyn instantly.

"Hey, Londyn." Starks walked over to his father.

"Welcome home young blood." B Starks had to be the coolest nigga alive. He never took his eyes off the newspaper he was reading when he spoke and gave is son some dap. "Say Slim, give us a minute," B said to Aunt Carla who was making everybody a plate of food. She took Londyn to the bedroom to watch TV. "Nephew, that mean fox just left here. If ya' auntie wasn't here boy, I might have tore it up." We all burst into laughter.

"Don't get shot, B." Starks had tears in his eyes because he knew his pops was capable of it.

B. Starks was smooth, he actually took one of Stark's women before. He looked good for his age. He looked like he was in his early 40's. The fact that he was cool as a fan helped him a lot. Aunt Carla knew how he was when she met him; she accepted everything about him.

She said she was too old to worry about B. As long as he respected her, she could care less about him being wit' a younger woman. None of them were a fourth of the woman she was. She was right; B had his fun with them, and made it home before 8 p.m. everyday.

"She's a brick house son. I don't know how he got her. Wait until you meet her," he said to Starks who was still recovering from the laugh we just had.

"She like that pops?" B nodded.

"Aight y'all need to get off my future wife. What up doe, Unc?"

"Ole Unc wanna smoke a joint wit' you young bucks." He pulled a half pound of weed from under the pillow that was beside him on the couch, along wit' more than enough blunts for us.

We sat there talking and smoking wit' B until my aunt came out of the room to get Londyn her nuggets. She walked into a cloud of smoke from the three blunts that were being smoked. She told us to air out her living room when we were done. I put towels by the door, so the smoke wouldn't get to her and Londyn.

By the time I finished my fourth blunt and my second plate of food I was right. I was ready to go apologize and chill wit' Cola. I said bye to everybody and kissed my sleeping beauty on the forehead.

I pulled up to the house at almost eleven at night. All of the lights were on except the bedroom me and Cola occupied. Her car wasn't out front; I wondered where she is. When I walked in, Jay was sitting on the couch talking on the phone. "What up doe bruh?" I greeted Jay.

"Let me call you right back." He ended the call he was on. "Shit. Go in that room and talk to that damn girl. She been walking around like a damn zombie all day. I told her to call you. She swear you about to leave her."

"She here? Where her car?"

"Kee got it. She went to Wayne's on 55th for some Orange Chicken."

"I should make her wait awhile longer before I go back there."

"Hell naw!!" Jay jumped up. "Go now. I can't deal wit' her when she depressed. Playing all them slow ass songs and shit. I was about to put her on suicide watch over yo' ass. Had me walking around here singing Jodeci all day because she had it on repeat."

"Aight I'm going, Jay."

Cola was sobbing on the bed when I entered the room. I hated to see her cry, but she was dead ass wrong for what she said. I was wrong for what I did, too. My anger got the best of me. Her back was turned to me when I sat on the bed.

"Co, I'm sorry I grabbed you like that and called you a bitch. You hit a nerve when you said that bullshit." She turned to me wit' puffy red eyes, I could tell she had been crying all day and half of the night. Seeing her like this had me feeling bad.

"I'm sorry, Baker. I was just mad at you for not coming home. I should have gave you a chance to explain where you were. My imagination was running wild. Dealing with Zell got me on edge Baker."

"You don't have to deal wit' him. I told you me and Jay can handle that. You, Kee, and, Londyn can go back to DeKalb tonight if you want to." I rubbed my fingers through her hair as she sat against the headboard with her knees up to her chest.

"No, I want to do this. I just have to get my emotions in check. You and him are two different men and I can't let this situation affect us."

"You sure?"

"Yes, I'm sure." I hugged and kissed her to assure her that everything was good between us.

"You forgive me?" I asked regarding me grabbing her. She shook her head. Our relationship had its ups and downs like everybody else's. Shit wasn't always perfect wit' us. It was gon' take a while for me to forgive myself for what I did to her. "Cool. I took Londyn wit' me to pick my cousin up."

"I know. I stopped by there after I picked my car up. I was supposed to go over there this morning, but Kee had to do a double at the hospital. I didn't feel like getting on the bus to go to Zo's shop."

"You could have had Jay drive the Maserati."

"I want to be extra careful now. Oh and I love your uncle, but if he cop another feel I'm telling Miss Carla."

"He a fool. He was talking about you earlier. Calling you a brick house." She smiled. "That's what I wanna see baby, that smile. I hate when you sad." I kissed her on her forehead. "I'm so sorry, Cola, I'll never do that shit again. I won't even point a finger at you."

She climbed on top of me and began taking my clothes off.

We had make-up sex all night. We fell asleep at seven the next morning. I woke up at noon to my phone vibrating on the floor. It was Starks.

"What up doe?...I was still sleep...Had a long night....Straight up?...You must have put in work wit' that judge if she reduced it to three months...Nigga that was too much information...I'll be over there in a few." I was happy Starks' house arrest was reduced. That meant he would be back on the streets helping me keep my affairs in order in no time.

"I don't feel good," Cola said as she wrapped her arm around me.

"What's wrong baby?"

"I'm nauseous. I think I ate something bad."

"What you eat yesterday?"

"Some jerk chicken and cabbage from that spot on Cermak."

"It was probably that cabbage, you gotta watch that. Everybody don't cook it right." She ran to the bathroom to throw up. I went in after her to make sure she was good. "You cool?" I asked while she brushed her teeth.

"I feel a little better."

"Chill for today. I'll go get Londyn and bring her over here for a couple hours."

"Bring me a ginger ale and some crackers on your way back please."

"I got you."

I took a long hot shower when Cola left the washroom. I laid socks, boxers, and a t-shirt on the bed. After putting my boxers on, I noticed a hole in the back of them. I got another pair; it had a hole, too. Every pair of boxers I owned had a hole in them. I unrolled my socks and noticed a hole in toe of both of them. I got another pair they had holes, too. After looking at 6 different pair, all wit' holes in the big toe I asked Cola, "What happened to all my socks and boxers?"

"Huh?"

"What happened to my socks and boxers? What the fuck? And my damn shirts?" Every shirt I owned had a hole in the underarm.

"That's what happens when you don't come home. Sorry." I

stared at her for a long time before I laughed. She knew what she was doing. Every time my socks and shirts had a hole in them I got mad. That got under my skin for some reason.

"You crazy," I laughed.

I picked Londyn up and dropped her off to Cola. I made my rounds to pick up my money, which was supposed to be done Sunday night. Being mad and off my square, I never picked it up. Before I went home, I went on 47th to get some shirts and socks. I stopped somewhere else to get some boxers. I'mma keep some in my car from now on, just in case Cola go crazy again. After that, I was in for the day.

Zell

Forgettin' my homie Boog was in the car wit' me I begin

thinkin' out loud. "I haven't talked to Cola in a few days. She won't return my calls. I wonder what that's all about."

"What you say?" Boog asked as we rode down his baby mama's block. He asked me to come pick him up because they had a fight. She pulled out a knife on him, let all the air out of his tires, and put sugar in his tank. That bitch was crazy.

"I ain't say shit. Ain't that Baker?" I squinted my eyes to get a better look. That was indeed Baker.

"Yeah that's him."

"What he doin' over this way?" He was sittin' in a Maserati talkin' on his phone.

"Probably pickin' up some money. He got some shit over here. That nigga makin' major bread."

"Yeah? We need to rob his ass."

"What you on? Baker good people. This the same person that put you on way back when."

"I don't give a fuck if he put me on. Look at the way that pinky ring shining. We can see that glare from a block away. He got money and I want it."

"Man you got money, too. Maybe not as much as Baker, but you got it. You don't have long money nomo' because you became careless. Spending all yo' cash on all them women you thought wanted you. You always got that good shit from Big Curt. When the money was short, he cut you off. You had to re-up with some shitty product." Silently I sat there agreein' wit' everything Boog said. I would never let him know that, though.

"Fuck all that, I want his money and I'm gon' get it." I pulled up right next to Baker. "What's up homie?" I said as he hung his phone up.

"What up doe?" He eyed Boog before he spoke, "What up Boog?"

I offered Baker the blunt I was smokin', he declined. I continued talkin' to him, "Tryin' to be like you and get this money."

"I'm the brokest nigga in the Chi," Baker said while I looked over at Boog who was textin' somebody on his phone. I wondered why he was so quiet.

"Shit Stevie Wonder could see through that lie." Lookin' at that ring on his pinky and the watch on his wrist was makin' me wanna pop him right here, right now. Lucky for him I didn't have my gun on me.

"Yo' I gotta go back to my girl's crib Zell," Boog said from the passenger's side wit' his phone still in his hand. Just as I was about to pull off, a green Ford Taurus sped down the block. Boog jumped out of the car and Baker sped off. I sat there confused until I heard gunshots.

Blocka, Blocka, Blocka.

Pow, Pow, Pow.

Blocka, Pow, Blocka.

My thoughts were, who the fuck was these niggas? And why they lettin' off on me? Just then my back window shattered. Speedin' down the street, I looked in my rearview, the car was gettin' close to me. I was out there naked wit' no heat on me. I couldn't defend myself.

Blocka, Blocka, Blocka, Blocka.

Pow, Pow, Blocka, Blocka, Blocka, Pow, Pow.

"Ahhh fuck!" I yelled as I felt hot lead from a .45 and a Desert Eagle pierce my left side, arm, and leg. "Fuck! Fuck!

Fuck!" I screamed as I looked at all the blood comin' from my side. I was gon' bleed to death if I didn't get away from these niggas fast. The .45 and the Desert Eagle were still bein' shot at me.

Blocka, Pow, Blocka, Pow, Pow, Pow.

Pow, Blocka, Blocka, Blocka.

The car was right on the side of me. I made a quick right as a masked face and black hooded body emerged out of the back passenger's side window wit' an Ak47. I saw a small manicured hand about to pull the trigger and tear my head off.

A bitch? What beef this bitch got wit' me? I checked my mirror to make sure I lost the car. I ignored all the pain I was feelin' when I jumped on the Dan Ryan Expressway on 55th street. I needed to go to the hospital bad, I was losin' a lot of blood.

When I looked up in my mirror, I saw the same green Taurus. These mufuckas was gon' shoot me on the expressway. Swerving from lane to lane, I tried my best to lose them until traffic came to a standstill. The large amount of blood I was losin' had me feelin' weak. With the Taurus exactly one car behind me in the lane to the left of me there was nothin' I could do. A nigga was a sittin' duck. Whoever this bitch was, she had the perfect opportunity to kill me if the lane their car was in moved before mine.

Slowly, the left lane began to move. I looked in my side mirror as the Taurus pulled up right next to me. The front passenger was lookin' right at me, wit' a 9mm pistol on his lap. I couldn't see the female in the back that had the AK. What I was about to do could cost me my life if the three bullets already in me didn't.

Sizin' up the small gap between the Taurus and the small Dodge Neon in front of it, I eased my car up close to the car in front of me. My lane of traffic began to move, so did the left lane the Taurus was in. I quickly swerved and crashed into the median that separated the expressway from the Red Line Train.

I woke up 8 hours later in Mercy Hospital. The Doctor came to speak to me and so did the police. I wouldn't tell them nothin'. They left their card for me to use when I was ready to talk. I balled the card up and tossed it on the floor, ain't no way I was tellin' them shit. The pain began to come back, I pressed the call button for the nurse to come give me somethin' for this pain.

When she came, I asked for my phone, I needed to call Cola. She walked over to the chair that had a bag with my property in it. She handed me my phone with a shattered screen. "Damn!" I yelled, startlin' the nurse. "My bad. I didn't know my phone was broke, I needed to call somebody to come up here wit' me."

"No worries, the bullets didn't cause any major damage. You will be out of here soon." She sounded muffled through the mask she had on.

"Why you got a mask on like I got a deadly disease or somethin'?"

"I think I'm coming down with a cold. I don't want to get any of my patients sick."

"Oh, a'ight." I spent the next week recovering in the hospital. When I find out who was in that car, I was gonna make sure I did so much to them that they would have to be cremated.

***

Three months had passed since I had been shot. I hadn't heard from Cola at all. I couldn't get another phone because the bill was in Anaya's name. She never added me as an authorized user nor would she go get me a phone. Dirty bitch. My credit was so fucked up I couldn't switch companies. I just said fuck it and paid a deposit to get a new phone.

I laid low while I tried to figure out who shot me. My car was fucked up, I was drivin' a rental whenever I had to make a run. I got tired of that and went out and bought a new car. I had a doctor's appointment set for today because the bullet in my side couldn't be removed. The Doctor was concerned because the bullet shifted.

I parked my new red Audi A8 next to a clean ass car. I had to give it to whoever owned that car, they picked the perfect color. Just as I was about to get out the car, I saw Cola walkin' out of the hospital wit' Kee. They were comin' directly towards me. When I heard the doors of the Maserati next to me unlock, I knew it was her car. I wondered what happened to that Range she was pushin' last time I saw her.

"What's up, Cola?" She turned around towards me and rolled her eyes. I knew she was probably upset about not hearing from me. That wasn't my fault, though.

"Hey," she said that dry as hell, like she didn't want to acknowledge me at all.

"Damn, why you say it like that? I got shot a couple months ago. The screen on my phone got cracked, I didn't have a way to get in touch wit' you." Her facial expression never changed while she listened to me explain myself. Kee never said anything to me. I didn't know what was wrong wit' these bitches. "You been aight?"

"Yes I have. Who shot you?" she asked as she started her car.

"I don't know. I'mma find out, though." Kee smacked her lips like I was lyin' or somethin'. "Damn Kee, you think I'm playin?"

"Nope." Kee was actin' like a bitch. She better be lucky I hadn't told Cola about her hoe ass.

"Anyway Cola, take my number and call me later. What you doin' here? You good?"

"Kee had an appointment." She locked my number in her phone and told me she would call me. If not later today, tomorrow. I watched her drive off tryin' to figure out how she got money. Two hours later, I was out of the clinic and on my way to holla at Boog.

"What's up?" Boog said as he walked up to my car. Boog

knew who shot me that day. I had a gut feelin' he was in on it. He was in a rush to get back to his girl's crib. To be honest, I think he gave them mufuckas our exact location. Nobody knew where I was that day.

"Shit, just slidin' in on you. Ain't seen you in a minute."

"I been chillin'. Where you been at?"

"Layin' low. After I got shot, I stayed out the way."

"I tried to call you a couple times. All I got was the voicemail."

"Phone took one for ya' boy. Shattered my screen. You heard anything about who shot me? I heard it was somebody I know. And why you lookin' around so much?" I lied to see how he would react. He looked from left to right at least ten times.

"Naw, I ain't heard nothin'. I just thought I saw that Taurus roll down the block a couple times."

Boog was nervous as hell while we were talkin'. Nigga was lookin' around every ten minutes and sweatin' like a Hebrew slave. Now I know he had somethin' to do wit' that shit. Baker pulled off fast that day, too. Baker a street nigga, his instincts must have told him to leave. I was ready to pull out my 9 and rock him to sleep.

"On that note I'll get up wit' you later. Be careful nigga, you never know who out to get you," I said as I made a U-turn.

My own guy set me up, damn. Fuck him. I'mma see that nigga real soon.

Cola

"Kee, I can't believe this."

"I can. I'm mad. As soon as we walked out of there we run into that jackass Zell. I can't stand that clown."

"I can't either. You see I couldn't pretend today."

"Are you going to tell Baker?"

"Tell him that I saw Zell or what happened at the Doctor?"

"Both."

"I definitely have to tell him I saw Zell. That visit with the Doctor caught me off guard. That was unexpected." I pulled up in front of the house, Baker's car was there along with a red Benz. "Who car is that?" I pointed to the unfamiliar car.

"I have no clue."

Weed was all that could be smelt when we entered the house. Jay was on the couch with his feet kicked up on the table. There was a black Polo jacket next to him that I know didn't belong to him or Baker. Baker was sitting in a chair next to the living room window.

"Baker, I need to talk to you."

"What up doe?"

"In the room." As we passed the bathroom, I heard the toilet flush and water running. I closed the bedroom door, so we could have even more privacy.

"What up?" he asked.

"Guess who I saw today."

"Who?"

"Zell. He told me he got shot and he didn't have a way to contact me, that's why I haven't heard from him. He gave me his new number."

"Straight up? I thought Kira was gon' kill that nigga that day."

"I wish she would have killed him." I know that was mean, but it was the truth.

"But I got other news." I took a deep breath not knowing how he was going to react to the news. "I'm pregnant." Baker just stood there, I couldn't read him. I wanted to know what he was thinking at the moment. A knock on the door brought him back to.

"Yeah?" he said to whoever was on the other side of the

door.

"I gotta go handle some things cuz. I'll holla at you later."

"Aight."

"That was your cousin?" I asked.

"Yeah."

"I guess I'll get to meet him another time."

"Yeah you will. Back to you being pregnant, how far along are you?"

"Ten weeks." I wanted another baby by Baker, but I wanted us to be married before I popped another baby out. Having one baby by him and not being married was cool, but two was too many for me. Being labeled as a baby mama was not in my plans.

"Baby, I want my Jr. bad, but it's not a good time for you to be pregnant."

"Hold on, what are you saying? You want me to get rid of it?"

"What? Hell naw! This shit wit' Zell gotta be done before you start showing, Co."

"I seem to start showing late when I'm pregnant. I promise it will be done."

"Aight. This better be a boy. Y'all women can't dominate the house."

"You don't want another little me?" I pouted.

"Hell nah I don't. You and Londyn are too much for me. Both of y'all always in my pockets getting whatever y'all want from me. I need somebody to be on my side."

"Forget you then." I waved him off. I wished my mother was here. She would be so excited about the new baby that was soon to come. I could see her angelic smile and feel her warm embrace.

"You a'ight?" Baker noticed the sadness in my eyes.

"I was thinking about my mother. I miss her so much Baker. She would have jumped up to go shopping as soon as I told her I was pregnant." Baker held me in his arms as I thought about my mother. He never said a word. He knew at that moment I only needed to be held.

"You cool now, Cola?"

"Yeah baby I'm cool. I don't think we should tell Jay yet."

"Why not?" Baker adjusted the volume on the TV so he could hear me better.

"Because he act like I'm paralyzed when I'm pregnant. I can't use the bathroom without him being right outside the door."

"Jay just paranoid about what happened to you. He don't want it to happen again. That's why he more protective of you when you pregnant."

"I just don't want to be babied right now." Thinking about the precious life currently growing inside of me brought a smile to my face. I really hope it's a boy, I wanted to give Baker his Jr. Him and Jay would love a little boy running around everywhere. Honestly I would, too. "I'm excited about the baby."

"Me too. I won't tell Jay," Baker said as he caressed my flat stomach.

"So, what's up with Boog?"

"Shit I don't know. I haven't talked to him since Zell got shot."

"Don't you think you should be checking on him? You said

you saw the nervousness in him that day. Zell might have saw it, too, and caught on."

"You right." I watched as he pressed Boog's number in the keypad on the phone.

"What up doe...You all good...He slid on you...Get you, yo' girl, and yo' kids shit together. Grab enough money to last a few months...I'mma have Cola go kick it wit' him, that way I know he won't see nothing...Nah, leave yo' car exactly where it's at....I'mma hit you and let you know when I'm on my way to pick y'all up." Handing me the phone he said, "Cola, I need a favor from you."

"I'm on it. He know about Boog, huh?"

"Yeah man. You mind if I let them use yo' old car while they gone?"

"They can have that car. I love my new car, what I need that old Impala for? Anyway we have four cars, one we don't even use that often," I said referring to the white Bentley that was sitting in our garage in DeKalb. I don't know why Baker bought that car. We only used it when we went to fancy restaurants. Which was rare because we preferred places we could relax and be comfortable in.

"Check you out just giving cars away," he laughed. "You got it like that? You can just give a car away like it's a dollar?" He yanked the covers off my nude body. Instantly, I felt the chill from the air conditioner.

"Must you play with the covers? It's cold in here and yes I got it like that. My baby is the man in the streets."

"I bet I can take you from him." Baker stood over me while I was still lying on the bed.

"He will kill you for trying."

"Fuck that bitch ass nigga."

Baker dropped to his knees, spread my legs, and ate his favorite dessert. In this case, I guess it was dinner and dessert. After he feasted on me, he penetrated my love tunnel like only he could. Baker hit every spot without trying.

"I loo----oh-----I love you!!!" I screamed as I had my fourth and final orgasm of the night.

Baker stood up with his chest poked out. "Now what you say about yo' man?"

"Fuck him." I kissed Baker's soft lips like I would never kiss him again. "I'm about to call him baby." He nodded. I got my phone off the night stand and searched for Zell's number, he answered on the third ring. "Hey what are you doing...You too busy for me...Meet you there in an hour."

"Where you meeting him at?" Baker called out from the bathroom located in our bedroom. He started the shower for me like I do for him in the morning when I wake up before him.

"Up North. Baker, I be tempted to stab him when I'm around him. It's hard to pretend that you like someone that has caused you and the people you love so much pain."

"Put yo' game face on baby, this how you wanted to do it. Text me as soon as you get there. Matter of fact don't text me, hit Kee up. When you around him and you want me, go through Kee. He don't need to accidently see yo' call log or some shit and stop thinking about stabbing niggas, crazy ass," Baker laughed.

"Alright."

I dropped the sheet that was wrapped around me to the floor. Stepping into the shower, I let water moisten every part of my body, even my hair. The warm water relaxed me almost as much as the sex Baker and I just had. I wanted to go to sleep, but there was a task at hand for me.

Thirty minutes later, I was pulling my wet hair into a ponytail. Walking to the closet, I pulled out some blue jeans and a white tank top. I refused to get all dolled up for a man that I despise.

My favorite scent, Luminous Touch, filled the room as I sprayed my clothes. I put on my white and silver T-strap sandals and my white gold necklace with a heart shaped diamond pendant and matching ring, Jay gave me for my birthday last year. Grabbing my keys, I told Baker I would be back in a few.

Pulling up to Zell's building, I pulled my iPhone out immediately texting Kee that I made it. I called Zell after to let him know I was downstairs. Exiting my car, I strutted to the building's entrance to find Zell standing by the elevator.

"You look good, Cola." He pulled me close for a hug. I hated the way his arms felt around me. It's hard to believe I used to love this muthafucka'.

"Thanks," I smiled. The elevator ride was silent the whole ride up. "So, what's new?" I asked as we entered his apartment.

"Shit I think Boog set me up. He was actin' all jumpy the day I got shot. Even when I saw him today he was nervous."

"I don't think he would do nothing like that."

"You would be surprised what niggas would do, Cola. You can't trust nobody, my own guy shitted on me." Well I'll be damned. That was exactly how Baker, Kee, and I felt when we found out what he did. "Just because I killed his brot..." Catching himself, he stopped talking in the middle of his sentence. Zell never admitted to killing Duke to anyone besides Tara.

Boog wasn't a true street nigga like his brother Duke. Boog mostly focused on the money. He was one of the nicest people I'd ever met. Unfortunately, almost everyone around him took his kindness for weakness.

"Whoa Zell. You killed Duke?" I asked as if I didn't already know the answer. "What would make you kill Duke?"

"Keepin' it one hundred, he knew somethin' about me that I didn't want to get out and the fact that I did some shit to him that he didn't like."

"What did he know and what did you do?" Hearing what Zell did from someone was one thing, him actually admitting it was another.

"I set somebody up." Zell was speaking on being behind Baker going to jail.

"Who?"

"The nigga that called me the night them hoes made you lose my seed. His name Baker." This man really said that like he wasn't the reason I lost my baby. It took everything in me not to slap the dog shit out of him.

"Why did you do that to Baker?"

"He was too comfortable, Cola. Always somewhere wit' a bad bitch or somewhere countin' money while everybody else was takin' all the risks. I started to hate that nigga, shit I still do. He still on top and I want it. He better hope I don't find out who his bitch is. I swear I will kidnap her, make him pay the ransom, then kill both they asses."

Listening intently, I looked at him with shock plastered on my face. I couldn't believe he was telling me all of this. Guess that was what happened when you lose all of your friends due to your grimy ways. I peeked down at my phone to make sure it was still recording. I snuck and pressed the button as soon as he had that slip of the tongue. "Don't you think that's a little extreme? What does his girl have to do with anything?"

"Guilty by association." I knew then that we had to deal with him sooner than later. If he found out I was with Baker, I would be dead before Baker could attempt to save me.

"Wow. Now, what did you do to Duke?"

"I don't want to speak on that."

"You mentioned it. You don't have a choice."

Zell let out the longest sigh before he spoke, "I hit his girl."

"What girl?" I asked with raised eyebrows.

"Come on, Cola. That's some old shit."

"I want to know."

"Damn, it was Kee. Before you start trippin' her pussy wasn't as good as yours."

My ears had to be deceiving me. There was no way I heard him say he slept with my best friend. I trusted Kee with my life, yet she betrayed me in the worst way. Some things you just don't do. It happened years ago, but I felt pain like it was yesterday.

Wait a minute, did this nigga just try to justify that shit by saying her pussy wasn't as good as mine. I can't fathom the fuckery of this fool right now.

"Muthafucka I should stab the fuck out of you and watch you bleed to death." Anger kicked in, I picked up his lamp and threw it directly at him. Instead of his head, it hit the wall.

"My bad Cola."

"Fuck you! You bitch ass nigga."

"Damn you the one that wanted to know who the fuck it was. I tried to switch subjects." A picture frame hit him in the mouth instantly making him bleed. "This the second time you made me bleed. You better chill wit' that shit."

"Foul muthafucka. You and that bitch Kee."

"Bitch don't act like you innocent. You know that wasn't my fuckin' baby. That's why I had the lil bitch stomped outta you." Rage filled my body. Turning around, I ran to his kitchen to get the biggest knife I could find.

He was right behind me yelling, "What the fuck you think you finna' do?" I was able to get a knife before he grabbed me by my waist flinging me into the stove. Hitting my head, I managed to keep a hold of the knife as I fell. I hid the knife under my body.

"Sick bitch. Why would you say that to me? That was my baby." I began to cry.

"Fuck that baby. You was gon' stab me, Cola? Huh? Is that what you thought you was finna' to do?" When Zell got close enough to me I stuck the knife in his left upper arm. "Fuck!! Ahhh!!" he roared. "Bitch, I got somethin' for yo' ass. I let it slide last time, but not this time."

Zell grabbed me by my ponytail and dragged me across the floor to his bathroom. I noticed he had a mop in his hand. He yanked me up by my hair and pulled me into his bedroom. Throwing me on the bed, he turned his back to me. I tried to run until I heard the sound of a gun cocking back.

"Get yo' ass back on that bed. Take yo' pants off first." I was about to tell him I wasn't about to do shit, but when I saw him screwing the silencer on his gun I knew to keep my mouth shut. I didn't know what he was capable of. "What the fuck you waitin' on?" I slowly peeled my pants off. I thought about my unborn child, said a quick prayer, and then got on the bed. Tears were falling from my eyes due to my fear of the unknown. I didn't know if he was going to kill me, beat me, rape me, or all of the above. "Don't cry now. Yo' ass wasn't cryin' when you stabbed me."

"Zell, what you said to me hurt. How did you think I was going to react to you telling me you had sex with my best friend?" Talking my way out of this seemed like the only option. It couldn't hurt, either Zell was going to let me go or do something to me I would remember forever, if he didn't kill me. "I still have feelings for you. Did you think that wouldn't upset me?"

"Talkin' yo' way out of this won't work. Open them legs nice and wide for daddy." Trembling as he pointed the gun at my head, I spread eagle. Zell wasted no time shoving that mop handle so far in my pussy I felt it in my head.

"Ahhhhhhhh, Zell please stop!" He kept ramming it as far as it would go. The pain was becoming unbearable. "God please help. Somebody help," I cried. Zell took the handle out of me, then shoved it right back in.

"God can't save yo' ass and if you scream help one more time, I'mma stick this gun above yo' asshole and blow you another one. How it feel Cola? Tell me it feel good."

"It…I…it feel…go…Ahhh!! Ahhhhh!!!! It feel good Zell! Please stop!" I could have sworn he just rearranged my insides. How could I have ever loved this crazy son of a bitch? He had a smile on his face the whole time he pushed and pulled that mop handle in and out of me.

"Is it better than my dick?" he asked while staring at me with demonic eyes. I closed my eyes wishing this was a bad dream. "I said is it better than my dick?" This time he asked louder. "Open yo' fuckin' mouth." Zell stuck his gun in my mouth, "Answer my question."

"Noooo it's, it's not better."

"It's not better than what?"

"It's not better than your dick." After ten minutes of enduring the pain of this mop handle, Zell was finally done with me. All I wanted to do was make sure my baby was okay. The thought of losing another baby because of Zell was my biggest fear.

"I bet you won't pull that shit again. Will you?"

"No," I said through sobs.

When he left the room, I ignored all the emotional and physical pain I was feeling. Putting my clothes on, I left the room and ran to the door. I picked up my phone and keys from the floor, I was close to the door. His voice made me stop dead in my tracks, "I'mma call you later, Cola."

This fool really was crazy. I have heard many things about the stuff he did to women. Never did I think I would experience it firsthand. Zell was a sick, twisted individual. Never in a million years did I think he was capable of doing something so vicious to me.

My stomach began to cramp very bad while I was driving. I called Baker to tell him to meet me at the hospital because I couldn't make it home in the amount of pain I was in. I drove to Rush University Hospital. I was rushed to a room after I started to bleed.

Baker

"Damn, Kee, slow this bitch down!" I said as Kee whipped her red Mustang GT through the hood like she was on the expressway.

"You can't handle a little speed?"

"I can, but you tryin' to get a muthafucka pulled over out here. Them people be low key out this way." My phone rang letting me know I had a phone call. I answered the phone for Cola on the first ring. "Aye make a U-turn and go to Rush, somethin' happened to Cola."

We got to the hospital in less than fifteen minutes thanks to Kee and her need for speed driving. I stopped at the lobby to find out where Cola was located. When I saw Cola in the hospital bed with messy hair and IV's in her arm, I had murder on my mind. Not to mention her head had a big ass bandage on it.

"What happened to her?" Kee said as she removed the gauze and examined Cola's head. Cola had a big open cut on her forehead. I'm not an emotional nigga, but it fucked me up to know somethin' happened to her and I wasn't there to protect her. "It look like she got hit with something." Kee was used to analyzing these types of things wit' her being a nurse and all. "You think Zell did that to her?"

"I know he did. He always doing crazy shit to women. I don't know what Co saw in him."

"He never showed her that side of him. Not saying that's the reason she stayed. Their relationship never got physical. He cheated and disrespected her, but he never put his hands on her." Kee sat in a chair across the room. I pressed the call button for the nurse, she came within seconds.

"Is everything okay?" she asked looking past me to look at Cola.

"Yeah. I pressed the button. I wanted to know if you could tell me what happened to her."

"Well Mr...."

"Wallace."

"Mr. Wallace, she would not tell us what happened. She came in with severe abdominal pain and a gash on her head. After an examination the Doctor could see that she had several small tears in her vaginal wall. We believe she was hit in the head with some sort of object. It also appears she was raped." I felt numb hearing my girl got raped. "She had a small tear on her cervix. We were able to close it with a stitch. Her and the babies will be fine. I hope she decides to tell us what happened to her. We need to get this maniac off the streets."

"Raped? Babies?" I asked.

"Yes Mr. Wallace. I'm sorry this happened to her. We had to conduct an ultrasound to make sure everything was okay. The technician believes he saw two fetuses. You guys will find out for sure when she has her next ultrasound."

"Thanks," I said as I went back to Cola's bedside.

"We gave her something for the pain. She should wake up soon. If you need anything call Nurse Cookie." I nodded at the nurse.

"Call Jay." I felt like this was my fault. I'm the one that had her go over there so I could get Boog and his family out of their house. I knew I should have grabbed my pistol, went wit' Co, and shot the nigga. Instead I almost cost my unborn it's life.

"Already did. He on his way."

I dialed Stark's number, he answered on the first ring. "Man, cuz, Zell raped my girl...I'm at Rush wit' her now...She pregnant...Nah they say the baby good…He gotta get dealt wit' as soon as possible…Straight up...A'ight I'mma hit you when she wake up and tell me what happened." I hung up wit' Starks just as Jay entered the room.

"What the fuck happened to my sister?" he yelled at no one in particular. Kee explained everything the nurse told us. "She pregnant? The baby cool?"

"Yeah the baby good, Jay," Kee told him.

"This nigga raped my fuckin' sister, Baker! He got me and the game fucked up if he think this shit here gon' fly!" Jay looked at me wit' an evil glare, "Is his mama still breathing?"

"Yeah she is, but she innocent Jay."

Jay pointed to Cola. "So is she." Jay had a point, but Vee had nothing to do with this. She didn't even talk to Zell because of his street affiliation. Vee was a diehard Christian and I refused to let Jay touch her. Killin' women wasn't his style, he was a lil hot right now. When he calmed down he would come to his senses. Our issue was wit' Zell only.

"I understand that Jay, but she don't fuck wit' him. He wouldn't give a fuck if you killed her. Zell a heartless nigga that don't care about shit."

"She saved her own life by not dealing wit' her punk ass son. I can't wait to make the nigga bleed. Me and you gon' be there when it's time to take care of the problem."

"Soon bruh, soon," I said as Cola opened her eyes looking around at all of us. She started crying when she saw all of us in the room.

"Baby, what happened? What that bitch ass nigga do to you?" I fired off as she calmed down.

"We was talking and he admitted to killing Duke and some more shit. I asked him how he got to Duke and he said through his girl. I asked him what girl and he tried to brush my question off. He finally said it was Kee." She gave Kee a death stare when their eyes met. "After that, he admitted to having something to do with me losing my baby and I went off. I stabbed him in the shoulder and he got pissed. He started talking about this being the second time I drew blood from him and he was gon' teach me a lesson. That's when I saw the mop in his hand…" Cola broke down crying as she relived what just happened to her. When she stopped talking, I made eye contact wit' Jay. This nigga raped my girl wit' a mop. What type of sick shit is that?

When Co got herself together you could see the emotion change from sadness to anger as she looked at Kee. "Kee, I trusted you and you went behind my back and fucked Zell when we were together. You dirty, trifling, no good bitch." Cola addressed Kee without so much as looking at me and Jay. "He told me about it. You supposed to be my muthafuckin' friend." I waited for Kee to say somethin'. All she did was buck her eyes and open her mouth wide. Jay looked like he wanted to beat her ass. "You don't have shit to say, Kee? Nothing? You just gon' sit there like a bump on a log looking stupid?"

"Cola, what you talking about?" I asked. Cola told me to grab her phone off the tray and listen to the recording. We all listened to everything that was said. Tears came down Kee's face when the struggle between Zell and Cola began. Jay punched the wall when he heard a muffled sounding Cola screaming for God. One of us had to remain calm, so I fought wit' myself to keep my composure.

"That's what I'm talking about. How could you do that to me, Kee?"

"Did I hear him right? He said he gon' call you later? What type of shit is that to say after what he just did to you? Zell gon' be a memory real soon," I said to Cola before I erased the recording. There was no need to keep it. I didn't want her to relive that ever again.

"Kee, you fucked that nigga?" Jay asked Kee. She still had her head hung low. "Did you fuck him?" Jay was standing directly in front of Kee wit' his fists balled up. Knowing he wouldn't hit her, I stayed next to Cola.

"No! I can't believe you would believe that, Cola. You and I have been through so much together. Your family took me in when I was young, so I wouldn't have to live somewhere where I wasn't wanted. Can't you see he trying to play you against me? Ever since I went off on him at that picnic he's had an issue with me and what other nigga would I be crying to him about? I was with Duke the whole time Zell was around. I know it's a confusing and stressful time for you, but don't get so caught up that you forget what's real and what's not."

"Whatever, Kee. I don't want to deal with you right now." Kee looked confused, hurt, and embarrassed.

I was getting ready to ask Co was she a'ight, but I didn't get the chance to ask that because as soon as her eyes opened, the pistol was going off. She shook her head no.

"Did he hit you in the head wit' somethin'?"

"I hit my head on the stove when he threw me on the floor. Baker I thought he was about to kill me. He stuck a gun in my mouth. I was so scared." To hear Cola say he stuck a gun in her mouth made my blood boil. Zell crossed a line wit' this shit here.

Through clenched teeth I said, "Trust and believe I got somethin' for him." I sat on the bed and held Cola in my arms to ensure her that she was safe. Jay left the room without saying anything to anybody.

Kee ran after him, but not before she said somethin' to Cola. "I'm sorry this happened to you. I hope you believe that I would never betray you like that. Hopefully, we will talk when you get well."

"Cola, I believe Kee."

"Baker, why would he lie about that?"

"Tell me you playing? Zell caused you a tremendous amount of pain in the past and now in the present and you gon' believe him over yo' best friend? Kee was right, you losing sight of what's real. Tell me the truth, did he do this to you or did you fuck him and do this shit to yourself so I won't be mad at you?"

"Really Baker? You accusing me of some bullshit like that? I'm laying here with a fucked up forehead, in a substantial amount of pain, and trying to be strong for our baby and you accuse me of lying? I don't believe this shit." I believed he did this to her, but I needed to teach her a lesson. Trust was everything in relationships. Whether it was friendships, family, business, or any other type of relationship.

"I'm just saying, you never know who you can trust."

"You don't trust me? If you don't, then we don't need to be together." Cola fought back tears.

"Maybe you need to ask yourself if you trust yo' best friend. How did me accusing you of lying make you feel?"

"It hurt me. We been together for a long time. One thing I know we have is trust."

"Kee been around longer than I have. Imagine how you made her feel. Baby you should have had a one on one conversation wit' her, instead of just coming at her like that."

Cola let out a sigh, "You right."

***

I spent the next two days at the hospital with Cola. Her and Kee made amends while she was still there. Kee and Jay straightened things out between them the same night they left the hospital. Everybody was back on track now.

"Thank you for everything, Nurse Cookie," Cola told her nurse as she signed her discharge papers.

"Oh, no don't thank me, Mrs. Wallace." Nurse Cookie winked at me. "You remind me so much of my daughter. If you need anything and I mean anything don't hesitate to call here for me."

The few days that we were at that hospital Cola and Nurse Cookie became very close. Cola was drawn to her because she reminded her of her mother. Nurse Cookie was drawn to Cola because she reminded her of the way her estranged daughter used to act. It was like mother and daughter being together again when I watched them interact wit' each other. Jay even had a bond with the nurse, he never got close to anybody without testing them first. There was somethin' about this nurse that had everybody in love wit' her.

"Nurse Cookie, how about we get lunch sometime?" Cola asked before Nurse Cookie left the room.

"I would love that." They exchanged numbers, hugged, and said their goodbyes. We stopped at Chef Luciano, on Cermak, for some Chicken Alfredo. Twenty minutes later, we were home.

"How you feeling? You comfortable? You need anything?"

"I'm fine, Baker. You think Londyn will be happy about having a brother or sister?" Cola was balled up under the covers. I looked over at the wound on her forehead, anger became evident on my face. I wanted to give Zell a slow, painful death. He deserved that shit for what he did to Cola. "Did you hear me, Baker?"

"Yeah my fault. I was thinking about some shit. I think my lil lady gon' be cool. I hope they don't have that obsession wit' ice cream like her."

"Nurse Cookie told you? I wasn't going to say anything until I knew for sure."

"Yeah, I figured that's what you was doing. It's all good

though it don't matter if it's one, two, or three, as long and they're healthy, everything will be cool." I pulled the covers back to lay down next to Cola. I hadn't held her the way I wanted to in a few days. I wrapped my arms around her and pulled her close to me. Kissing her on the forehead like always. "I hope it's two boys."

"A girl and a boy you mean."

"No more girls." Truthfully, I was scared to have girls. I would kill a nigga if he did anything to hurt my daughter. I know I'mma have to put a lot of boys in their place over Londyn. She was a lighter version of Cola. I couldn't take going through that with two girls. I wanted nothing, but boys from now on.

"First we have to see if it's more than one in there. Then we will worry about what we will name our daughter or daughters." She snickered. I didn't know if she was hiding it or if she really was cool, but she seemed to be her normal self. Cola was the epitome of a strong woman.

"One of them gon' have to stay with my aunt," I told her as I reached for my vibrating phone. It was Starks. "What up doe...She good...She got you, too, I see...Come through in the morning...Aight." I set my phone back on the night stand. "Yo' daughter got my cousin out buying cookies and ice cream."

"Everybody falls in love with my mini me. It would be nice to meet him, Baker. He is around my daughter a lot now."

"Get some rest, you will meet him tomorrow."

"Goodnight."

I kissed her on the forehead. "Goodnight."

Within minutes, Cola was sleep. I stayed awake for another hour just thinking about what Cola went through. I hated that I let her go into the line of fire. I loved this woman to death. Zell hurt her and that meant he hurt me. My face would be the last face he saw before he met the man that made him.

What type of man rapes women, let alone do it with a mop? That shit was foul. I felt myself getting angrier wit' each thought I had. Tempted to go to his house and kill him in his sleep, I decided to close my eyes and go to sleep. I couldn't leave Cola right now, but I wanted to be the one to kill him or at least be there when it happened. I pulled Cola closer to me and fell asleep.

I wonder if she called the police on me. Fuck, I should have just beat her ass and called it a day. I needed somethin' to take my mind off this shit. I searched the table for my phone. When I found it, I called Peachy to come over.

As I waited on Peachy, I hoped and said silent prayers that the police wouldn't come kick my door in. One thing I never did, was show Cola my violent side. She didn't know I had issues wit' women or had a so called disorder. I never took my Lithium the way I was supposed to cause wasn't shit wrong wit' me. Couldn't no Doctor tell me I was Bi-polar.

Bein' molested by my own mother fucked me up bad. Now she was all God fearin' and whatnot. This bitch even married to a preacher. She wasn't praisin' the Lord when her hands was down my pants or when my dick was in her mouth. Nobody knew the real reason my mother didn't talk to me was because I knew her fucked up secret.

Valencia, known to others as Vee, was a heroin addicted prostitute when I was growin' up. She would shoot up and come in my room on nights she didn't have a trick over for the night. I stopped takin' showers to try to get her to stop. I even purposely didn't wipe my ass good, so the smell would make her leave, but she kept right on. On my thirteenth birthday, I put an end to it.

Vee came in my room that night, crawled in my bed, and put my hand on her breast. I moved it, she didn't care. Her hand was makin' its way down to my boxers. Her head disappeared under the covers. I clinched my fists when she put my limp dick in her mouth. When it wouldn't get hard, she stormed out of my room. I jumped out of my bed to get the pot of scalding hot water I was boiling.

Carefully takin' steps, I quietly crept to the bathroom she was in. Vee was sittin' on the toilet wit' a needle in her arm when I pushed the door open. I threw the big pot of hot water on her before she could look up. From that day forward, I never had to worry about her comin' in my room. I left her house a year after that happened. I wonder how her preacher husband would feel about her secret.

I wasn't capable of trustin' women. I only saw one purpose for them, sex. Cola was different from other women that I'd met. For some odd reason, I loved her. That was why she never saw my violent side. Usually, I would walk it off when it came to Cola. This time, I showed her who I really was. To be perfectly honest, I didn't feel bad. The time apart made me lose some love for her. I did still love her, though.

"What's up?" Peachy sat on the couch and crossed her legs.

"Just wanted to chill wit' you."

"You ain't talked to Naya?"

"Fuck that bitch. I don't have shit to say to her." Just like Cola, she was pregnant wit' another man's baby.

"For why?"

"Because I don't."

"That night I had met her, she was real upset 'bout you. She was callin' and textin' you, but you ain't never get back to her."

"I never got her calls."

"Well ionkno' why you ain't get 'em. I seen her call log." I need to hurry up and put my dick in her mouth. The way she talked was ridiculous. I knew I didn't talk proper, but damn somebody need to send her back to elementary school.

"Oh, well, that's old shit anyway. Do what you do best, Peachy."

Without sayin' anything Peachy fell to her knees and pleased me like only she could. I ended up fuckin' Peachy without a condom again. I wanted to pull out, but the pussy was too good. Peachy put me to sleep.

I woke up hours later to an empty house. Glancin' on the floor next to my shoes was a piece of paper wit' a smiley face on it. Curiously, I eyed the paper for a few minutes. Finally, I picked it up and unfolded it. It was from Peachy. I read it silently, then again out loud.

"YOU JUST CAUGHT THE AIDS FROM ME!! PAYBACK A BITCH!!!!"

My heart skipped a thousand beats. That couldn't be true. Peachy didn't look sick, shit she looked damn good. That bitch just mad I shot her. I didn't have time for this bullshit ass game she was tryin' to play wit' a nigga. If she had it, then Naya had it. She hadn't called me and told me she had it. *Fuck she can't call she don't have my new number*. I decided to call her. Dialin' her number, I put the phone on speaker so I could roll a blunt.

"What?" she answered on the fifth ring.

"That's how you greet mufuckas that call you?"

"Nigga, fuck you. What do you want? It's taking a lot for me not to come burn ya' bitch ass alive."

"What you wanna do me like that for?"

"You playing dumb now bitch? Have you been giving me money to keep myself up until I replace your ass?"

"Man, I ain't fuckin' you. Why would I give you money?"

"Oh, yeah?"

"Yeah bitch."

"Because you are the reason my life is fucked up."

"What? You trippin'."

"Where in the fuck did I get HIV from? You sick dick having bitch. I hate you. I hope you drop dead today. You gave me a disease I can't get rid of. Not only that, I could die from this shit. What if I give it to your son? Huh? Don't call my phone again. Don't let me see you in the streets."

"Shut that shit up. What you gon' do if you see me?"

"Stab your bitch ass." Naya hung up leavin' me wit' my thoughts.

How did this happen? What the fuck? These hoes probably on some get back type shit. Her and Peachy gotta be in on this together. They just fuckin' wit' a nigga head. My thoughts were interrupted by the ringin' of my phone.

I looked at the screen and saw the hospital's number. "Hello...this me...naw fuck that...it ain't true...you mufuckas think this a game...don't call my phone wit' that...calm down, shit, bitch...bye."

Is this, fuck up Zell life day? I took a pull from the blunt. I wanted to kill everybody right now. That phone call had me heated. I tried to call Peachy. Her phone was disconnected, which was strange because I had just called her on it hours ago. That dirty bitch better not ever let me catch her in traffic. I'mma kill her on sight.

Pussy was literally gon' be the death of me. Dr. Hughes confirmed I tested positive for HIV. I know I was a fucked up individual, but damn did God have to get a nigga back like this?

Since Zell attacked me, I'd been doing okay, thanks to Baker. I was upset and hurt about what Zell did, nonetheless I refused to let it get me down. My babies were my reasons for staying strong. As long as them and Londyn were good then I was cool. Zell was a sick individual. He had to have a mental problem to do something so vulgar.

For two weeks, Baker hadn't left the house. He was there to comfort me if I needed it. I fell asleep in his arms every night and woke up with them still wrapped around me. I felt so safe with Baker. I never knew love like this existed in real life.

Every day he asked me if I needed to talk or wanted to get out of the house. He ordered me flowers once a week just to bring a smile to my face. Baker was making me fall deeper in love with him by being there for me the way he was.

This morning I was up making us pancakes, sausage, eggs, and grits for breakfast. Baker walked in the kitchen wearing a pair of basketball shorts. I couldn't help but admire his toned body. Especially his six pack. Lord have mercy my man was blessed.

"You cooking? How much money you need?" Baker sat at the table waiting for me to bring his plate.

"Shut up, I don't need or want anything. I haven't cooked in a long time. You been here with me day in and day out making sure I was okay, I thought I'd repay you."

"That's my job as yo' man, to be there for you. My main priority is making sure you good. I'm supposed to be there for you no matter what. Any man would do this for the woman he loves." He took a bite of his sausage. "Thanks for cooking baby. I get tired of eating Kee burnt food."

"Fuck you!" Kee yelled when she ran past us out the door to go to work. We both laughed.

Baker took another bite of his sausage. "She got some supersonic ass ears. Ain't no juice in there?"

"We got some fruit punch." I poured him and myself a glass. We sat at the table and ate breakfast together.

"Man, Cola, I'm sorry." Baker had been saying this to me every day, more than once. I knew he felt bad about what happened to me. He expressed that he felt it was his fault. He wasn't at fault. It's not like he knew what was going to happen to me that day.

"Stop telling me that. I told you it's not your fault. None of us expected something like that to happen. Our babies are fine and so am I. Now, I want to forget about what happened."

"I need to do somethin' for you to make me feel better. What you want? I feel like I failed to protect you."

"Nothing Baker I got everything I need. You didn't fail, it's not like you were there and didn't do anything. You weren't there, therefore you didn't fail to protect me."

"My point exactly, I wasn't there. Now, what you want?"

"In this case you couldn't be there, but since you putting pressure on me I want you to take me shopping."

"Damn. When?"

"Today." I laughed at his facial expression. Baker hated shopping with me because I had to go in every single store. Even the ones I knew I don't want anything out of. That was what he got for pressuring me.

"I should have left well enough alone." The doorbell rang, Baker got up to answer it. I stayed in the kitchen to wash dishes. I could hear him and whoever was at the door talking in the living room.

"What up doe?"

"Put a shirt on before you answer the door cuzzo."

"You ain't nobody."

I didn't get a chance to meet his cousin the last time he came over because my pain pills had me out of it. Baker yelled for me to fix his cousin a plate. I fixed the plate and took it to the living room. Only the back of their heads were visible when I walked up.

"I feel some kinda way about you sitting so close to me without a shirt on." Baker moved closer to him to mess with him a little. I let out a small laugh behind them. Both men turned around to face me. I damn near had a stroke when I saw who was sitting next to Baker.

"Thanks baby." Baker took the plate from me and handed it to his cousin. "Cola, this my cousin, Starks. Starks this my girl, Cola."

"Nice to meet you." Starks acted as if he had never seen me before. That was fine by me. Right now I didn't need any drama. We can play this game forever for all I care.

"Yeah, it's nice to finally meet you, too," I said as I eyeballed Starks picking up his fork and begin to eat. Uncomfortable wasn't the word for how I was feeling at the moment.

Of all the people in the world why did they have to be cousins? My heart was skipping beats as thoughts from my past began to float around in my mind. I didn't know what Baker would do if he found out about Starks and I. More than likely he would leave me. The thought of not being with Baker hurt me. I knew the reality of it would kill me.

Baker grabbed me and guided me to his lap. Talk about awkward. He kissed me on my cheek and forehead before he told me told me he would be ready to take me shopping in an hour or so. Starks didn't look our way, he pretended to be deep into the TV. I caught a glimpse of him looking at me out of the corner of his eye. At that instant, I wanted to jump off Baker's lap and run like a bat out of hell.

After getting dressed, I went downstairs to finish cleaning up the kitchen while Baker was in the shower. My mind had to be playing tricks on me. They can't be cousins. When I peeked in the living room, Starks was still sitting there. Lord help me.

"Where you want this?" Starks asked holding the plate I had given him.

"I'll take it." When I reached for the plate I almost dropped it. My hands were so shaky and sweaty. Being near Starks had my nerves going haywire.

"It's a small world, Serenity."

"Yeah, it is." I avoided eye contact with Starks.

"You don't have to be nervous around me. I'm not gon' tell him about us."

"How can I not be? In the past I cared about and slept with the cousin of the man I want to spend the rest of my life with. If Baker ever finds out I don't know what he would do."

"The only way he will find out is if you tell him." His eyes always talked to me. They told me he was confused. We had a conversation about me leaving Zell a few times. Starks went to jail before I could act on our conversation. I never told Kee how serious I was about Starks. Kee was convinced it was just sex.

"You too close to my girl Starks." Baker joked with Starks when he walked in the kitchen.

"Pops is the one you need to be worried about, not me." The two cousins laughed.

"You ready for this long journey we about to go on Co?" Baker asked me while he adjusted his red and black Chicago Bulls fitted cap on his head.

"Of course I am. This is all your fault. Had you left me alone earlier we wouldn't have to go," I smiled at Baker who had a fake frown on his face.

We all headed out of the front door. Baker wanted to take his Range because he knew I would have a lot of bags. When Starks got in the back of the Range Rover my nerves got the best of me. My palms were sweaty and I was very uncomfortable. Why couldn't he drive his own car?

My stomach was in knots while Baker and Starks talked during the drive. Baker stopped his conversation with Starks to tell me he had to make a stop. Baker turned the volume up on the sound system. Rick Ross's song *Triple Beam Dreams* came blaring through the speakers. Riding around with Baker would make a deaf man hear again. His music was always turned up to the max.

We were on 67th and Western at the same auto shop that painted my car. I was relieved when they both got out of the car and walked into the shop. Starks turned around and looked at me before he was all the way in the door. It's crazy how your past could come back to haunt you.

Starks pulled out of the shop minutes later in a silver Camaro. Baker got in the Range and we headed to the mall. Most of the ride was silent. You would have thought Starks was still in the car by how quiet I was. I felt really bad about not telling Baker about Starks. Being scared about how Baker would react, had me keeping my mouth shut until further notice.

"What you wanna do for yo' birthday?" Baker asked as we rode around the mall parking lot looking for an empty parking space. We parked close to the entrance of the mall. My twenty-sixth birthday is less than twenty four hours away. I wasn't excited about it. It wouldn't be the same without my mother. I don't really want to do anything special this year.

"Whatever Londyn wants to do."

"Hell nah. I'll send y'all to get y'all nails done or somethin'. We all can grab somethin' to eat when y'all done. That night I'mma plan somethin' for you. That cool wit' you?"

"That will work."

Our first stop at the mall was the candy store for Londyn. We spent at least forty dollars on candy. Miss Carla and B are gon' put it up for her to have in moderation. We got ourselves a stash, as well. Baker brought me everything from gym shoes and sandals to dresses and shorts. He spent a few hundred dollars on Londyn a summer wardrobe. He bought himself some shoes, clothes, and fitted hats. We took all of the bags we accumulated to the car before we went back in the mall to do more shopping.

"Where you wanna go next?" Baker asked.

"You should know where I'm trying to go. I want some new scents and underwear."

"Cola, you better be lucky I love you." Baker shook his head because he knew I was going to use his arm to test the scents and ask his opinion about bras.

"I just spent three hours picking out hats with you. Now that's love."

Baker laughed, "I was in and out of there in thirty minutes."

"Still too long to be looking at hats. You bought about ten hats for that big bald head."

"You don't be saying that when you be kissing on it."

"Because I love it."

"You ain't gotta tell me that, I already know. Let's hit yo' store up."

After spending about forty minutes, smelling scents and picking out underwear, I was done. Baker paid for all my stuff before we walked next door to another clothing store. Baker looked in the Polo section first, then he walked to the section where more men's clothes were. Jake was there with some dark skinned girl that looked like she had a stank ass attitude.

"What up doe, Jake?"

"What's good fool? What's up, Cola?" Jake spoke to both of us.

"Hey Jake," I said with a smile as the girl looked me up and down. Just as I suspected, she had much attitude.

"Spending some much needed time outside the house wit' Co today."

"That's what's up. Yo' Baker I need to holla at you." Jake didn't introduce us to the girl he was with. I didn't know why she looking at me all nasty like I did something to her. She walked over to another section of the store before I could speak to her. Fuck her then. I brushed it off and listened to Baker and Jake's conversation.

"What up?"

"Do you still need me to keep her around?"

"That's Anaya?"

"That's a headache. I can't take too much more of her. She would be cool if she wasn't money hungry. Goo told me you needed to get away for a minute. Everything all good?"

"Nah, you can get rid of her. Everything cool, shit got a lil hectic. I needed to chill wit' Co at the crib for a minute."

"I feel you on that. Check this out, though, Zell gave her HIV."

"Stop it!" Baker said in disbelief, as he picked up a pair of jeans. Shock and sorrow was plastered all over my face. Despite the fact that she was giving me much attitude, I felt bad for her.

"I wouldn't play about that."

"Damn Zell is the true definition of a savage, straight up. She pregnant right?"

"Nope. All she wanted was some money out of Zell. She told me that out of her own mouth last week. All she about is money."

"How you find out she had HIV?" Baker and Jake looked through the stack of jeans. I glanced over at Anaya, she had one hand on her hip and the other playing with her weave.

"I found out she had that package 'cause I was chillin' at her crib one night, right. The nigga Zell called her, so she go to the bathroom. I heard her yellin' 'bout some bread he ain't give her or some shit. He must have said some slick shit to her cause all of a sudden I heard her say tell me where the fuck I got HIV from and how he fucked her life up. I'm sittin' there stuck not knowin' what to do."

"Nigga you bullshittin'." Baker gave me four pair of jeans to hold while he and Jake moved over to the section for shirts.

"Dead ass serious, Baker."

"That's crazy. Did she tell you she had it?"

"The only thing she told me about was the fake pregnancy. That same night after I heard her on the phone she started talking about what she wanted to do to me. I pretended like I was gon' fuck her just to see if she would tell me she had it. She was goin' to even after I said I didn't have a rubber. I told her I practice safe sex only and left her on the bed in her panties."

"Doing shit like that gon' get her killed. She can't be playing wit' nobody life like that."

"That's what I was sayin' to Goo. She need to tell niggas and let them make the decision about whether they want to take that risk or not. I'm about to take her home. Baker, I'mma holla at you tomorrow. Cola take it easy." Jake walked off and Baker put his arm around my neck while we walked towards the register to pay for his items.

Often times, I asked myself what did I do to deserve a man like Baker. He was every woman's dream. Baker treated me like a queen. He gave me the right amount of attention and affection. Spoiled wasn't the word for how he had me.

Baker paid for my mother's funeral when she passed. Jay could have done it himself, but Baker wanted to show me that my mother meant just as much to him as she did to me. He also wanted to show me how much he loved me. He even paid for me to go to school to become a Surgical Technologist. Baker told me from day one, he wanted me to have something to fall back on just in case anything ever happened to him. I didn't think there was a man on God's green earth that could compare to mine.

When we left the mall, it was dark outside. I was beat, we still had one more stop to make for Londyn. Baker wanted her to have a shopping cart with the groceries and a kitchen set. Baker pulled up to Miss Carla's house at about nine at night. I saw Starks's Camaro parked in front of us. I was uneasy about going in at first. My daughter was inside the house, so I had to deal with it.

I searched the back of the Range for Londyn's clothes, candy, and toys. When I had everything, I handed Baker a few bags to carry. My hands started to shake and my heart started racing due to the fact that Starks was inside the house. Another thing that bothered me was that he was around my daughter. Not that Starks was a bad person. I would rather Londyn not be around someone

I had a sexual relationship with other than her father.

"Mommy!!! I wanna sleep with you mommy. You got a sowe." Londyn gently rubbed the scar on my forehead.

"Hey my baby! I miss you so much. My sore is almost gone baby girl."

"It hurt mommy? I wanna go with you."

"It doesn't hurt anymore. You can come with me, but you have to come back tomorrow."

I picked Londyn up to go speak to Miss Carla and B in the kitchen. Miss Carla almost had a heart attack when she saw all the candy we bought for Londyn. Meanwhile, B was picking through it getting what he wanted. Baker walked past the kitchen to the back room. I assumed it was the room Starks was in.

I talked to Miss Carla for a few minutes. Baker hadn't come out of that room yet. I started to peek at the door like that would help me hear something. I was worried Starks would tell Baker everything. I didn't want to be around Starks and I didn't want Baker to be around him alone. I was in a bind that I didn't know how to get out of.

I asked B to go get Baker because I was tired, plus Londyn had her Dora bag ready to go. He came and told me that Baker said go wait in the car and he would be out right behind me. I sat down at the table and waited.

"I thought you was waiting in the car?" Baker said twenty minutes later.

"I knew better than to believe you would be right behind me."

"Impatient ass. I wasn't back there that long." He took Londyn off my lap and headed towards the door. Everybody said their goodbyes to each other. Starks came out of the door with us along with three duffle bags.

"Where he going?" I asked while I watched Starks pack his car with the bags. I didn't care where he went as long as he wasn't coming back to Kee's house with us.

"Presidential Towers. He had a crib there before he got locked up. I pulled a few strings and got him his old crib back. I have to stop and pick this money up. You riding or going home?"

"I'm going with you daddy," Londyn said from the back of the car. I looked back at her and smiled. She loved taking rides, no matter how short or long, Londyn loved being in the car.

"I guess we riding with you daddy," I mocked Londyn.

"That turned me on. Say it again." Baker turned to look at me and bit his bottom lip. He put his hand on my thigh and rubbed just a little.

"Our daughter is in the back seat." Londyn was in her own world looking out of the window.

"She ain't paying us no attention. Give me some of them sexy ass lips while we at this light." I leaned over to give Baker a kiss on his full soft lips.

"You nasty mommy. Daddy didn't bwush his teeth when he woke up at Uncle B house." Londyn had me in tears.

"That was a long time ago lil girl. I didn't have a toothbrush over there. I brushed them when I got home," Baker said as he glanced in the rearview mirror and smiled at Londyn.

"Okay, daddy okay."

"She just dismissed you, Baker," I laughed.

Baker shook his head and laughed. "This what I mean about

y'all women dominating the house. They gotta be two boys."

Pulling up on 27th and State Street, Baker called his friend Goo to let him know he was downstairs. We sat in the car for about fifteen minutes before Baker called Goo again. He told him he had me and Londyn in the car with him. Apparently the money was short and Goo was trying to figure out what went wrong. Goo came downstairs five minutes later with four bags from a shoe store. Each bag had two pairs of shoes in them with money rolled up inside the shoes.

"Uncle Goo!" Londyn said as he gave her a ten dollar bill. Goo gave her money every time he saw her.

"Hey Cola and Little Cola."

"Hey, Goo. Tell Kira to call me. I haven't seen her since his party." Goo's girlfriend Kira is cool. We went out together a few times, she was a ball of fun.

"No good Cola, we broke up a couple days ago."

"What?"

"I'm playing, she back there with her sister having a cocktail. You should go back there and chill with them."

"Boy stop playing with me. Maybe next time, Goo. We been out shopping all day, I'm tired."

"A'ight, I'mma tell her to call you tomorrow." He directed his attention to Baker. "One of them young cats felt like his pay wasn't enough." Baker and Goo had to talk in codes because they didn't want Londyn to hear anything.

"How much overtime did he do?" Meaning, how much money did he take.

"Three stacks worth."

"You docked his pay for that?" Baker was asking what punishment did Goo give the young boy. He didn't believe in killing people for minor things. However, Baker wanted whoever crossed him or tried to cross him to be reminded of what they did or tried to do. Stealing was something Baker hated. When someone came to him with the question of how to handle a thief the answer was given in the form of the question, can a man with no hands steal?

"Definitely."

"Cool."

"I still ended up terminating him. He started talking reckless after I docked him." Goo had to kill the boy. The look in Baker's eyes told me he felt bad about the boy losing his life. At that moment, my love for Baker grew even more. The compassion he showed for the person's life that stole from him was admirable.

Most niggas in the hood wouldn't care. Baker was a rare breed. He wasn't a bitch by far, but he wasn't ruthless like the average man in the streets. Baker only killed when necessary, not just because he had the power to do it. He was in a league of his own in the streets.

"Come on Goo, don't tell me that. Could that have been avoided?" Baker turned his key to start the car.

"Trust me it had to be done. He was talking about getting our families."

"That type of talk ain't tolerated. Hit me when you done wit' all this."

"A'ight, Baker. Happy early birthday Colaaaaaaaaaaaaaaaa!" Goo screamed. He had everyone outside looking in our direction.

"Awww, thanks, Goo." Goo told me to tell Kira whatever I had planned, he wanted to be there to celebrate with me. I assured him I would let her know. Goo disappeared back inside of the building.

Fifteen minutes later, we were getting settled at home. Londyn was running around the house with Jay. Baker was in the kitchen making Londyn a hot dog and fries, and I was in the bedroom putting away everything we bought at the mall. After Londyn ate and had a bath, she fell asleep in the middle of our bed. Baker and I showered together before we called it a night.

Am I really about to ask her to marry me? I questioned myself while I was lying next to Cola in bed. I knew I wanted to marry Cola a long time ago. Now that the time had come for me to ask the question, a nigga was shittin' bricks. I got the ring from my Aunt Carla's house when we picked Londyn up. I talked to Starks and B about it for a minute. Starks said go for it. B told me finding the love of a good, loyal woman came few and far between.

I rolled over to look at the clock. It was almost time. I didn't really think this through to be honest. All I put thought into was the ring and when I wanted to do this. My nerves had me ready to smoke one before I popped the question. Fuck it I might as well smoke.

I carefully crept to the kitchen to get my half smoked blunt from the ashtray. After hittin' it a couple times, I was good. Before going back to the room, I looked at the clock one last time.

At midnight I nudged Cola, "Wake up baby."

"What's wrong?" she asked wit' sleep in her voice.

"Nothing, I need to holla at you." She looked at me then at the clock. "No, it can't wait." I answered her question before she asked it. I already knew when she looked at the clock she was gon' ask could it wait until we got up.

"Baker, I'm tired," Cola said sleepily.

"Happy birthday beautiful."

Cola gave me the ugliest frown, "Thanks. That better not be what you woke me up for."

I laughed, "Nah, it's not. I love yo' ass man. You and Londyn are my world. I can't breathe without y'all, straight up. Cola, you every real nigga's dream. You cook, clean, always looking out for me, and you don't ask for shit. Probably because you just go in my pocket and take it. You gave me a beautiful daughter and about to give me another lil one or two soon. You crazy, but yo' crazy ass is worth the risk of possibly being stabbed." After she playfully hit me in my arm, I continued to talk, "I'm not perfect, but I wouldn't be shit without you. I love you, Serenity. Will you marry me?" I unraveled my hand to show her the ten carat, princess cut ring I picked out wit' the help of Jay.

"Oh, my God!! This ring is beautiful, Baker. I love you so much!! I can't wait to be your wife." After I put the ring on her finger, she gave me the tightest hug and the longest kiss. "Baby, you know what I loved about that proposal?"

"What's that?" She still had her arms wrapped tightly around my neck.

"It was real. Not some Hallmark version of what you wanted to say. Only you would say, 'you every real nigga's dream' and curse in a proposal. Just so we're clear in my eyes you are perfect. Ahhhhh!!! I can't wait to show my ring off. I have to go tell Kee and Jay."

Cola ran to Kee's room first. All of Kee's screaming almost woke Londyn up. I went to her room and told them to calm down before they wake her up. Kee and Cola ignored me while Kee admired Cola's ring.

Jay burst in the room right after me. "What the hell y'all doing all this screaming for man? People trying to sleep around this bitch."

"We getting married, Jay." Cola held her hand out to show Jay her ring.

"Sis, you think I don't know that? Who you think went with him to pick out the ring?"

"Jay! Why didn't you tell me?"

"Girl you trippin'. I wasn't gon' ruin my brother's surprise."

"Oh, so you about to forget about me because you have a brother now?"

Jay looked at Cola and then at me. Wit' a serious tone he said, "I been had a brother. This been my brother since I saw how good he treated you and how much he loved you."

"I thought you was a real nigga, Jay?" I joked.

"Says the nigga that just handed his dick over. You sure you wanna do this, Baker? You know that girl ain't all the way there sometimes."

"Don't get slapped, Jay," Cola said through laughter.

Jay put his hand on my shoulder. "See what I mean. She

violent. She gon' beat on you, Baker. It ain't too late to take the ring back." Jay ducked to avoid getting hit wit' the pillow Cola threw at him. "On some real shit, though, congratulations."

It was about six in the morning when everybody went back to sleep. Londyn woke everybody up three hours later. Cola made breakfast and cleaned up. After she was done, I gave her some money to do whatever she wanted. Two hours later her, Londyn, and Kee were out the door.

"That fuck nigga Zell ain't called yet?" Jay asked me after the door shut.

"Nah bruh. He might know he crossed the line for real this time. I heard that nigga got HIV."

"What the fuck?" I told Jay about the conversation I had wit' Jake at the mall. "Shit, we need to speed this nigga's death up then. Bitch ass nigga violated my sister wit' a mop like she ain't shit."

"Don't remind me about that shit, Jay."

"Man we had that nigga on the E-way that day. Kira got a mean shot. I should have sent her instead of Marlene that night."

"Probably should have. Kira is vicious wit' a pistol that's why Goo stopped cheating on her for a while. She put a .45 to his dick and threatened to take his manhood in broad daylight in front of us. She had my mans looking like a bitch on 64th and King Drive in front of everybody."

"Kira a muthafuckin' gangsta."

"That's why Boog wanted her wit' you and Jake that day."

Three months ago Boog called and said he was ready to get his revenge on Zell for killin' his brother, Duke. Boog stayed close to Zell to make it easy whenever he decided to get even. It was a real slow move for Boog, but he finally made it. He said he waited so long to retaliate because he wanted Zell to think he got away wit' killin' Duke.

The thing that puzzled me was the fact that Boog didn't want Zell dead. If I had a brother and a nigga killed him, you better believe he gon' die as soon as I found out about it. I didn't object to what Boog wanted. I gave him my word that Zell wouldn't get killed, not that day anyway.

Boog made up a story about getting into it wit' his girl, so Zell would come pick him up. Meanwhile, I parked where I knew

Zell would see me. Boog called me when he got in the car. That was his signal for me to tell my people to get ready. Three blocks away, Kira, Jay, and, Jake sat waiting on me to call them so they could be on their way. I knew Jay would go against everything and kill Zell. For that reason, he had to be the driver.

Big Curt supplied the guns needed for the job. My quiet homie, Bubba, had a way wit' words when he did talk. He got us the old Taurus from a fiend for a $300 bundle of dope. It was nothing to part wit' a bundle to get this job done. When I saw Boog jump out of the car, I looked up to see Jay doing about sixty miles per hour down the block. I pulled off when they got close.

Jake and Kira handled their business like I knew they would. Kira had a vendetta against Zell based on the fact that Goo didn't like him. She would go to war against twenty niggas to defend Goo. Two of the three bullets that hit Zell were hers. Jake didn't know Zell like that. The things he heard about Zell made him despise him.

"Boog made the right choice. That shit was live. I never got the thrill of chasing a nigga I wanted to kill. They always bitch up."

"Kira said the same thing. She asked me who was next."

Jay laughed, "Kira is like one of the guys."

"Hell yeah she is."

After I got done talking to Jay, I went to take a nap before I met up wit' Cola. At about two in the afternoon, I woke up to check my phone. Cola hadn't called me yet. That meant I had time to take a shower, line, and trim my beard. I pulled the tags off a pair of black Levi cargo pants and a purple short sleeve button up shirt. The purple shirt matched the purple in my black grape Jordan 5's perfectly.

The scent of weed filled my nostrils while I sprayed my Gucci cologne all over my shirt. Jay stayed wit' some kill. He wasn't stingy wit' it either. I was trying to resist the urge to hit the weed. The smell was calling my name like that crack was calling Pookie in New Jack City.

"Check it out, Jay."

Jay appeared in the doorway wit' the blunt in his hand blowing smoke rings, "What's up?"

"We taking Cola to eat in a minute."

He passed me the blunt. "Them girls would have a fit if I leave outta here. I don't want them problems."

"I know you tired of being in this house."

"This shit kinda decent. I see why you do it when you ain't handling shit in the streets. Shit is peaceful." This couldn't be Jay talking. He used to be allergic to staying in the house. Now he talking about he liked it.

"Kee must have put that thang on you. Her and Marlene nurses. What you got a nurse fetish bruh?"

"Fuck you," Jay laughed. "It is somethin' about a woman in some scrubs that turn me on."

"You a fool. I wanted you to come out wit' us for yo' sister's day."

"Bring the party to me. Put on some Meek Mill, let's have a house party."

"That sound better than going to that expensive restaurant I planned on taking everybody to tonight. My plan was for everybody to get dressed up and go to The Signature Room on the 95th floor of the John Hancock building. I wanted to celebrate our engagement, her pregnancy, and her birthday in style."

"I ain't a suit type of nigga. Throw her a BBQ. Call Big Curt over to get down on the grill and you good. Cola don't want nothing more than what you already gave her."

"That's what it is then. Hit Big Curt up for me bruh. I'm about to call Kee and put a plan in motion."

Big Curt and Kimmy were already bringing grocery bags of food and liquor inside when I finished making all my calls. Big Curt jumped up as soon as possible to get things ready for the BBQ, since he loved to grill. Bubba volunteered to be the DJ. He pulled up wit' his equipment twenty minutes after I called him.

Big Curt had the grill going and Bubba had the music blasting. Everybody in my circle came to show Cola love. Goo and Kira was there, Nurse Cookie had her son drop her off, Aunt Carla and B came over, too. Starks said he would come through later. I had already hit Kee and told her to invite some of their friends that I didn't have numbers on. I also needed her to make up a reason to come home. All we were doing was waiting on them.

Cola was in the passenger's seat of Kee's Mustang when the car pulled up. Kee and Londyn came in the house while Cola sat in the car. Londyn ran to give me a hug, then straight to Jay. Goo picked her up and had her in the air like she was an airplane. She had the biggest smile on her face while he spun her around. Kimmy's sister was on her way wit' her kids so Londyn could have some kids to play with.

I felt someone grab my leg. It was Londyn. "Daddy look at my toes. Mommy mad."

"Those some pretty lil toes. I'mma go see what's wrong wit' mommy. Go play wit' uncle Goo." Londyn ran off to go find Goo. All I saw was the top of her curly ponytail bouncing through the kitchen.

Cola was sitting in the car wit' her arms folded when I approached. I opened the car door for her to get out. Cola stepped out wearing a pair of white shorts that had her ass looking plumper than I'd ever seen it look before. She had on a black sleeveless shirt that showed off the small pudge of her pregnant stomach. If you didn't know she was pregnant, you would think she ate a big meal.

I leaned on the hood of the Mustang. "Londyn just told me

you mad. What up?"

"Of all days, he picked my birthday to bother me, Baker. He got a serious problem. I don't understand why he texted me in the first place after what he did to me. Sick son of a bitch."

"What he say in the text?"

She read the text to me: *Happy birthday. I would love to spend the day with you. Let me know what's up.* "He act like he didn't attack me. No normal person would do that and act like everything is peachy." Her tears began to fall. She hadn't cried about what happened to her in a minute. I knew she was thinking about what Zell did to her all over again.

Pulling her close to me I said, "Stop cryin' I'mma take care of that nigga. Sooner rather than later." Cola looked up at me and I wiped the last tear from her face. That's when I noticed a red Audi wit' tints pass us by. It caught my attention because of how slow it was going down the block. I waited until it turned the corner before I walked Cola to the house.

"We still going to eat?"

"Nah, we can eat what's in the house," I said as I walked Cola in the house. I turned around to check out the scenery.

Somethin' didn't feel right to me.

"Baker, I want to go…What is everybody doing here?" Cola had a huge smile on her face when she saw everybody sitting around talking, drinking, and eating.

"They all here for you baby."

"Wait a minute…" Kira said, "…is that a ring on yo' finger?" All eyes were on Cola's left ring finger. She held it out for everybody to see. Kira, Kimmy, and the rest of the women surrounded Cola, and gave her hugs. The men clowned me for a while. When all that was over, they all congratulated me.

"That ain't the only news they got." Jake walked over to Cola and pointed to her stomach.

"AHHHHHH…" Kimmy screamed, "…we are gonna be pregnant together!!" *No wonder she ain't drinking*; I thought.

"Damn Big Curt!" We all said in unison. Big Curt and Kimmy had four kids together, three boys and one girl, plus Big Curt had two older kids from a previous relationship.

"She fertile than a mutha y'all," Big Curt said and we all laughed.

"Thank you everybody that's here to celebrate my birthday, my engagement, and my pregnancy."

"Our engagement," I corrected her.

"I heard that Baker. Y'all are a unit now," one of Cola's friends shouted.

"Excuse me then, our engagement and our unborn child."

Everybody yelled happy birthday and congratulations before mingling and making plates. Big Curt should have been a chef. The meat was so tender and juicy it fell off the bones. Everywhere I looked people were laughing and talking. The kids were outside having a water gun fight wit' B Starks and Goo. The rest of the guys were eating and smoking. I motioned for Big Curt to step into the kitchen wit' me. I needed to talk to him about that Audi I saw earlier, it didn't sit well wit' me at all.

"You know a nigga that copped a red Audi wit' tints recently?"

"Nah. Why? What's up?"

"I saw one when I was out there talking to Cola. It crept past slow as hell. It had tints and temporary plates."

"That could have been anybody."

"Somethin' telling me it wasn't just anybody. It was going too slow. It damn near came to a stop. Like whoever was driving it saw somethin' they didn't wanna see or they was looking for somebody."

"You see the girl over there on the couch?"

"Yeah, I see her."

"If anybody know who that was, she do. She know everybody business and got hoe tendencies. I'mma have Kimmy spill her drink. Hopefully, she'll come in the kitchen to get another one. Follow my lead."

We watched as Kimmy knocked the girl's drink over. Just like Big Curt said the girl was on her way to get another one. We pretended to be talking about somethin'. As soon as she got in earshot of the conversation Big Curt said, "I don't know. What's his name again? I need to check him out before he can do business with me."

"His name Zell."

"What he drive?"

"I don't even know."

"He drive a red Audi. He got that car after his car got shot up," the girl said. My gut told me somethin' wasn't right about that car. Now he knew about me and Cola. "I wouldn't do business wit' him if I was you."

Big Curt asked, "Why not?"

"He's Bi-polar. He just snap for no good reason, especially on women."

"How you know that?"

She took a long breath. "Zell is my brother."

Shock was all over both me and Big Curt's faces. Neither of us knew Zell had a sister. I had a thousand questions I wanted to ask her. I'd known Zell for years, he never mentioned having a sister.

"What's yo' name and who you come here wit'?" I took a long hard look at her. She resembled Zell a little.

"Jazzy. I came wit' Kira."

"Jazzy I knew Zell when I was younger. Why didn't I ever

see you around?" Jazzy looked uncomfortable about what Big Curt just asked.

"Vee was the worst kind of person. She used to be on drugs and would beat Zell when she wasn't out selling her pussy to every man that wanted to buy it. Our grandmother raised me when the state took me away from her because I was born addicted to crack.

They didn't take Zell for some reason. I wish they would have taken him. Vee molested him for three years. On his thirteenth birthday, he threw a pot of boiling water on her after she tried to suck his dick. He left a little while after that happened and never looked back. She really messed him up. I know what she tells people about him. I don't know what's worst, her lying about why she doesn't socialize with her son or her never admitting she has a daughter."

That was some heavy shit she just told us. Big Curt was sittin' on a barstool wit' his mouth wide open. I had my arms resting on the island in the kitchen. I met Vee through my aunt. I always thought she was nice, she fooled the fuck out of me. I couldn't believe she did all that shit to Zell. That would explain why he was so fucked up in the head.

"You still talk to yo' brother?" I asked.

"Nope."

"If you don't mind me asking, why y'all don't talk?" I figured she told us everything else, why not tell us that?

"I just found Zell a year and a half ago. I ended up staying with him and his girlfriend Anaya for a couple of months. One day, Zell came home and Anaya started on him. She knew how to push his buttons. I personally don't like her stuck up ass, but anyway, he just snapped and beat the shit out of her. I tried to stop him before he killed her. He turned around and started beating my ass. Zell told me to pack my shit and never come around him again."

Big Curt wanted to know, "If he called you right now what would you do?"

"I wouldn't give Zell shit on a popsicle stick. He accused me of stealing money from him and beat me up more than a couple times before he put me out. The whole time Anaya was the one taking his money. She watched him beat the shit out of me numerous times and didn't attempt to do or say shit. If I ever see her I'm spitting in her face and I dare her to do something about it."

"How you know about what Vee did to him?" I was curious to know.

"When I first found him, we were real cool. He told me everything that happened to him and admitted that he was diagnosed with Bi-Polar disorder. When he completely stopped taking his medicine, the problems began. I'm trying to save y'all from making a big mistake. I heard he set his own friend up before. Y'all seem like good people. If I can prevent my brother from fuckin' y'all lives up, I will," wit' that she walked back over to the couch where the rest of the women were.

"Didn't I tell you I had a feeling about that car?"

"You did. What you gon' tell Cola?"

"I don't wanna tell her shit. She gon' start trippin' when I tell her. I gotta sneak Londyn out of here. I know he gon' come back. Fuck he doing over here anyway?"

"Ain't no telling wit' that nigga. You ready for what might happen?"

"You ain't gotta question that."

Jake walked over to us wit' a cup of Hennessy and a plate of food. "Yo', Kira sister just walked in with a couple females and you won't believe who one of them is."

"Who?" I was curious to know.

"Go see." Jake shook his head.

Just as I was about to get up I heard a female yelling, "She just spit in my face! It took me an hour to do this make-up."

I heard another one say, "You damn right I did bitch. I dare you to do something about it." I already knew who was wit' Kira's sister. Jazzy stayed true to her word, as soon as Anaya walked in, she spit in her face. Everybody was watching the scene play out until I became the voice of reason.

"Jazzy, be cool aight?" I said to her in an attempt to calm her down.

"I'm sorry. I'll respect you and your house, but if she so much as open the car door too fast outside I'm beating her ass. I got my ass beat by my brother because of her, now it's her turn."

I didn't care what happened when they left here. They could kill each other for all I cared. As long as Londyn and the rest of the kids were here, they had chill. Kids imitate what they see. I was always careful about what I did and said in front of Londyn and the rest of the kids.

Curiosity was getting the best of me. I went to the kitchen where Kira's sister was and asked how she knew Anaya. She explained that she didn't really know her like that and she was a friend of her friends. They were all in the car on their way to get somethin' to eat when Kira called her over here for the BBQ. It was an innocent coincidence that Anaya ended up here today.

While still in the kitchen, I heard a loud thump then I heard Kimmy screaming for somebody to get Cola. I bolted to the living room where I saw Cola hit Anaya in her mouth wit' her fist.

Anaya raised her hand to hit Cola back. Before her punch could land, Cola hit her in her left eye knocking her to the floor. After Anaya fell, all I saw was Cola landing punches all over her. Jay stopped Kee as she ran full speed towards them. Cola didn't need backup she had it under control. Although she had the upper hand, the sight of her fighting had me hot.

Pregnant or not she didn't need to be fighting. I rushed over and grabbed Cola by her waist to stop her. Somebody else in the room should have thought to stop it before I did. I guess they felt that since Cola was handling hers it didn't need to be stopped.

Co was trying her best to get away from me. When she realized she couldn't, she gave up. Jazzy and Kira came from out of nowhere stomping Anaya while she was still on the ground. Big Curt and Goo had a hard time pulling them off of her. They did a number on Anaya real quick.

Kira's sister gave her friends a warning not to get involved. They stood there watching Anaya get beat up. Shit would have gotten ugly if they would have tried to help.

"What the fuck was that all about, Cola? You pregnant. Why you in here humbuggin' like this?" I was pissed at her for fighting while she was pregnant. Not to mention kids were in the house. They happened to be in the basement playing games wit' my aunt and uncle.

"Ask her why I'm fighting. This bitch came at me talking about I'm the bitch Zell left her for. Saying she about to beat my ass for taking her man and money away from her. She put her hands on me and got her ass whooped. Plain and simple." Cola was huffing and puffing while she explained everything to me.

"Yeah…" Kira added, "…she had to be dealt with, Baker. You don't come to nobody house and pull this type of shit. Cola enjoy yo' party. Fuck that ignorant ass hoe. You lucky they pulled me off you." Kira tried to kick Anaya. Goo met his match when he got wit' Kira. She would stand tall against anybody at any given time. She didn't give a fuck.

Starks felt bad for Anaya and honestly so did I. They fucked her up bad. He held his hand out for her to grab and said, "Get up, I'm about to take you home."

"Hold up, Starks." I called out before he made it to the door. He stopped and turned to me. "Be careful, I think we got eyes on us."

"You know I always expect the unexpected out here," he said as we walked further out of the house.

"I got a bad feeling somethin' gon' happen today. I wanna make sure everybody prepared."

"I'm good. Baker, trust me."

Out of nowhere somebody started firing shots at us. I didn't have a pistol on me, so I couldn't shoot back. I didn't have a choice, but try to duck and dodge.

Blam, Blam, Blam, Blam.

Boom, Boom, Boom, Boom.

Blam, Blam, Blam.

Boom, Boom, Boom, Boom, Boom.

Somethin' pierced my flesh before I fell to the ground...

Nicole Black, whose real name is Nicolette, was born and raised on the south side of Chicago. Her love of reading has always gotten her through tough times. During a rough patch, instead of reading she decided to write. After months of writing, Nicole passed her finished book around to close friends who urged her to get it published. Nicole loves tattoos and has a weakness for caramel. She is still a resident of Chicago where she is working and raising her son, Jamari.

Find the author on Facebook
https://www.facebook.com/nicole.black.1293575?fref=ts

Be sure to text SHAN to 22828 to keep with all the releases from Shan and the ladies of Shan Presents.

CPSIA information can be obtained
at www.ICGtesting.com
Printed in the USA
LVHW041755150519
617950LV00017B/901

3 1333 04850 2726